SUNRISE ISLAND CHRISTMAS

Sunrise Island Series
Book 3

Maren Hill

Chapter One

Emily Warren stood at the edge of the cliff, the brisk December wind biting her cheeks as she stared out at the sea. Below her, the waves crashed against the rocks, as restless as her thoughts. Sunrise Island glittered with Christmas lights, its charm and warmth pulling at her heart. But no amount of festive cheer could change the truth: in just six months, she would be gone. She had to be. Her father's addiction was swallowing her family whole, and even Nick, with his steady love and dreams of a future here, couldn't anchor Emily to this place. Not when her mother needed her across an ocean.

Emily turned toward the farmhouse, glancing at the barn as Nick led Music, Jennie's palomino, outside.

"Have a good ride," she called, waving as Nick slipped his foot in the stirrup and mounted the horse, whose breath puffed visibly in the frosty air.

"I can't wait to teach you how to ride, Em," Nick said, grinning. "Oh, and you might want to head into the kitchen—

Grandma's baking another batch of her famous shortbread cookies."

Emily had grown accustomed to the familiar delight in Nick's eyes whenever he'd spoken of Kathleen's baking. She watched as Music walked toward the open fields, gradually trotting before breaking into a gallop. Nick leaned forward, his body perfectly aligned, back straight and strong. Emily had dreamed of learning to ride since she was a young girl, her love of horses sparked by the movie *Black Beauty*. It had been her escape from a troubled childhood, where she imagined riding far away from a home that left her too embarrassed to invite friends over.

The aroma of freshly baked cookies filled the kitchen, wafting through the air as Emily swung open the door and stepped inside.

"Good morning, Kathleen," Emily said, even though it was already close to lunchtime.

"Good morning, dear," Kathleen replied, pausing her work. "A fresh batch will be ready for sampling in a few minutes. If you'd like to sit while the cookies cool, there's fresh coffee. I hope you don't mind the plain ones, by the way; they give the best taste of the shortbread."

Emily watched as Kathleen moved with confidence, swiftly and expertly shaping dough at the counter. "I don't mind at all," Emily chuckled, savouring the buttery aroma that filled Kathleen's cozy kitchen.

Emily couldn't help but feel a twinge of envy. *How does she make it look so easy?* Kathleen's kitchen exuded the warmth of years of tradition, a place where baking seemed like effortless magic. As Emily stood there, she couldn't help but think of her own failed attempts at making shortbread—the dough had always been too dry, crumbling in her hands until, after countless tries, she had finally given up.

Choosing a mug from the cupboard, Emily filled it with rich, dark coffee, and sat at the kitchen table. Wrapping her cold hands around the warm cup, she let the heat seep into her fingers.

Emily watched Kathleen pull a baking sheet from the oven and set it on a wire rack to cool. Her eyes drifted to the golden shortbread, wondering when it would be ready for tasting.

"Have you ever tried making shortbread, Emily?" Kathleen asked.

"Oh," she scoffed, "don't even ask, Kathleen. I would like nothing more than to figure out how to make cookies like these, but..." Her voice trailed off as she glanced out the window, watching a flock of pigeons land in perfect formation on the barn's roof.

She didn't need to finish—Kathleen's knowing smile said she'd heard it all before. "Well, if you're interested, I'd love to show you a few tricks. But first..."

Emily beamed as Kathleen placed three cookies, all different shapes, on a plate and set them in front of Emily. "Here you go, dear. See what you think."

Emily took her time, eyeing the smooth edges. She chose a cookie shaped like a Christmas tree, velvety soft between her fingers. *With a gentle press,* Emily guessed, *the cookie might give way.* Her eyes widened as the buttery, melt-in-your-mouth treat hit her taste buds. It was perfect—just perfect.

"Oh, my goodness," she said through a mouthful. "This is incredible."

Kathleen's eyes twinkled with the pride of a job well done. "That's the Mitchell family shortbread. Every year, people try to guess how I do it. But the secret stays right here." She tapped her temple with a playful wink.

Emily smiled, swallowing the last bit of cookie, but a wistful sigh escaped her. "I have tried making shortbread so many times, but I always get it wrong. My mum and I eventually gave up. Sticky toffee pudding is more our speed," she said, chuckling.

"Well, I'm sure your sticky toffee pudding is something to rival mine," Kathleen said, wiping her hands on her apron. "Though I do have a little idea..."

Emily blinked, curious. "Idea?"

Kathleen leaned in, lowering her voice conspiratorially. "I don't usually share this recipe—it's a Mitchell family secret, passed down for generations. But... you're not entering the Sunrise Island Bake-off, are you?"

Emily shook her head, laughing softly, her high ponytail swaying gently with the movement. "I think I'm safe from that."

"Good," Kathleen said, her eyes sparkling with secret delight. "Because I was thinking... since you'll be heading back to England, maybe I could trust you with my secret recipe." Kathleen's voice softened, warm as the cozy kitchen. "You can take a bit of Sunrise Island back home with you," she said. Then, with a twinkle in her eye, she added, "But I'll need something in return."

Emily's breath caught. Kathleen seemed serious. "Are you saying... you'd give me the recipe?"

Kathleen nodded, her eyes twinkling. "On one condition: You give me your sticky toffee pudding recipe. I've been trying to perfect it for years, and I'd love to know how the English make theirs."

Emily could hardly believe what she was hearing. "You'd trade your shortbread recipe for sticky toffee pudding?"

"I couldn't think of anyone I'd rather give it to, Emily," Kathleen smiled warmly.

"What do you mean, Kathleen?" Emily asked.

"A special gift for the woman my only grandson has fallen for," Kathleen said. "Besides, it's not like you'll be competing against me from across the Atlantic."

Emily's heart swelled at the offer. It wasn't just the recipe—it was the trust, the connection. Even though she had just met them, she felt welcomed into something special—the heart of the Mitchell family's tradition. *Does she see me as part of the family because I'm Nick's girlfriend?* Whatever Kathleen's motivation, taking a little piece of the island to England made her return feel... somewhat less daunting.

Emily smiled, feeling that sharing their sticky toffee pudding recipe felt like sharing a part of herself and her mother. "Deal," she said, feeling a lightness that transcended the turmoil she had felt only hours ago on the clifftop. "I'll write it out for you."

Kathleen beamed. "I'll do the same. But remember—my shortbread recipe is top secret. It doesn't leave your kitchen, okay?"

"I promise," Emily said, a hand over her heart.

"What's your mother's name?" Kathleen asked, opening a drawer and pulling out a small, worn recipe card.

"Charlotte," Emily said, "but everyone calls her 'Lottie.'"

"Such a pretty name," Kathleen said, handing the card to Emily as if it were something precious. "But no peeking before Christmas," Kathleen added with a wink.

Emily held the card gently, her warm brown eyes filled with gratitude. It wasn't just a recipe—it was a piece of the Mitchell family's Christmas magic. She looked around the cozy kitchen, her eyes resting on Kathleen, who had welcomed her with such warmth. A deep sense of belonging settled over her, something she had not expected to feel here, so far from home.

As Kathleen returned to the oven, humming a soft

Christmas tune, Emily drank her coffee, a sense of peace settling over her. Maybe returning to England didn't mean leaving everything behind. Maybe, with the Mitchell family's shortbread recipe tucked safely in her pocket, she would carry a bit of this place—this warmth—with her wherever she went.

Chapter Two

Emily was keen to see as much of Nick's world as possible before she returned to England in June. Even though they'd slept in and missed the sunrise at Sea Star Point Beach, it was still early when they arrived. With no one else in sight, they reveled in the serenity, imagining everyone else caught up in the frenzy of Christmas preparations.

"You're a hopeless romantic, Nick", Emily said, smiling, as she wrapped her arm around Nick's waist and pulled him close.

"Guilty," Nick agreed, "at least on the 'romantic' part. But I'm not giving up hope that you'll stay here with me after graduation."

Emily turned away, gazing toward the ocean. Then, her eyes full of fun, she turned back to Nick and said, "I know you think that Sunrise Island is the most beautiful part of the world, but I've got news for you. If you come visit me in England, I'll take some time off and we can travel around the coast."

With no reply from Nick, Emily persisted, "The UK has

some of the best coastlines in the world—Devon, Cornwall, Hampshire. If you like dramatic cliffs, medieval towns, and amazing beaches..."

But Nick didn't look convinced. "Sunrise Island has everything we need right here," he countered. "We can use this as our home base and travel anywhere in the world once we gain a solid footing here on the island."

Emily sighed, feeling her tactic had failed.

"Just give it some time, babe," Nick said.

Time... if only we had met at a different time, Emily mused, *when I didn't have to worry so much about my parents.*

"Sunrise Island will work its magic on your heart just like you've worked yours on mine," Nick added, making magic sound logical.

The vibration of her phone interrupted Emily's thoughts. Seeing her mother's name flash across the screen, she replied solemnly.

"Mum, we're out walking on the beach" she shouted, louder than she needed to. "I don't know if we'll stay connected, but what's up?"

Signalling for Nick to walk on while she took the call, she turned and walked in the opposite direction.

"I just wanted to hear your voice, Em," Charlotte said. "You know how it is. Christmas is hard for many people, and I needed to know you're within reach."

"Mum, I'm just a phone call away, you know that," Emily said, "but I'm glad you called to test it out, all the same."

"Thanks, Em. It's just weird being away from you over Christmas, that's all."

"I feel the same way, Mum. You're in my heart, always. Please call me anytime; no worries."

"Okay, love." Pausing, Charlotte added, "But what if you're out of battery? What if I need you right away?"

"Oh, Mum, please don't worry. If it's urgent, you can call the police, as you've done many times. And as soon as I see you've called, I'll call you back."

Silence was the only response on the other end of the line until Charlotte replied. "I guess so. You're right, Em, Thanks for the reassurance."

"You're welcome, Mum. These days it's easy to connect. Even though we're oceans away, I'm really only seconds away."

"Love you," Charlotte replied, sounding cheerier this time. "I'll let you get back to your walk."

"Talk soon, Mum. I love you too."

Catching up to Nick, Emily explained, "It was Mum. She just needed to know she could reach me when she wanted."

"I see," Nick said with a smile. "I guess it's hard for your mother, you being away at Christmas."

"That's right, but it's all good." But it wasn't all good. Her mother's voice still lingered, carrying the weight of a world Emily could not leave behind, no matter how much she wished she could.

Emily touched Nick's wrist, slowing his pace. "Do you mind if we check out that cute little shop next to the café?" I'd like to buy something Christmassy for our room—something for just you and me."

Nick laughed. "Ah, okay, sure. I never thought we'd need any more Christmas decorations at Cliffhouse, but I get the idea."

Just for you and me, Nick," Emily whispered, brushing a light kiss across his lips. But as she pulled away, Nick's warmth drew her back, wrapping her in a tender embrace. Her heart quickened as his soft, full lips melded with hers in a kiss that felt like it would last forever. The moment lingered. She closed her eyes, surrendering to his irresistible pull, the world fading until there was only Nick—only this.

...

Nick stood with Emily in his childhood bedroom, helping her stretch a homemade garland across the bay window. She had wanted something to remind her of the island and their time together.

After securing the garland, they both stepped back to admire it. "Oh," Emily said, "that's perfect. Small pieces of driftwood to remind me of the beach, sprigs of fir to remind me of your farm, and bright red hearts to remind me of you."

Nick felt a warmth spread through him at her words. "Em," he said with a grin, "we can string this up every year to remind us of our first Christmas at Cliffhouse."

Emily seemed thoughtful for a moment, but instead of asking what was on her mind, he tried to lighten the mood.

"Now," Nick said, "shall we head down to join Mom and Clay in the basement? They asked if we'd help sort the decorations."

"Of course," Emily agreed, her smile returning. "I bet you have lots of decorations for a big place like this."

Nick chuckled. "You have no idea, Em. The whole basement is storage for decorations. Traditions are a huge part of our family."

"Your grandmother told me the Open House is on Friday and it's an outdoor event. Do you decorate both inside and out?"

"You'll be amazed at how far we go," Nick said proudly. "It's not just a family celebration—it's for the entire island. And, judging by other years, that means pretty much everyone."

The basement door was already wide open, and Nick could hear his mom and Clay chatting as he and Emily stepped in.

"Welcome!" Clay greeted him, hoisting his drink can high in the air with a grin.

Nick caught Emily's look as she glanced around the cavernous space. "Woah, this room is massive, perfect for all these boxes," she exclaimed.

"Yeah, it seems organized now," Jennie said, but trust me, appearances can be deceptive."

Clay chuckled, already on Jennie's wavelength. "Case in point," he said, lifting a box labelled *Wreaths*. He opened the lid to reveal toys and gifts for the outdoor Christmas tree.

Nick smiled. "All part of the fun. Where would you like us to start?"

"How 'bout you two handle the outdoor decorations?" Jennie suggested. "Clay and I can take care of the inside."

"Sounds like a plan, Mom. What about Lexi and Kye? Will they be helping?" he asked.

Jennie laughed. "Helping as always, but not with this at the moment. Alex's braiding Music's mane and Kyla's in the kitchen helping Mom."

"And Patrick," Clay began, glancing at Emily—he's my son from Dublin—he'll pitch in with setting up the tables and the dance floor once he gets here."

Nick surveyed a towering stack of boxes. "Think we can get all this together in four days?"

Jennie gave him a confident look. "We always do, and we've got two extra helpers this year. We're already ahead of the game."

Nick grabbed a box marked *Outdoor Bulbs* and handed it to Emily with a playful grin. "Here, Em, see what you get. It might be bulbs, or it could be something entirely different."

Nick and Emily devised a loose plan for the outdoor setup as they sifted through the endless decorations—Christmas bulbs, garlands, wreaths, and ornaments. Nick loved how organized Emily was, matching candy cane to candy cane, toy soldier to toy soldier, but he soon realized she'd keep going without a break if he didn't intervene.

"Time for a break," he announced, stretching his back.

Emily shot him a look, half-amused. "I'm just getting started."

"I know you like to work straight through, Em, but we do things differently here. Farm life taught us that breaks are essential. Besides, I'm making Mexican hot chocolate for everyone, or if you prefer, a spiked one... your choice."

"No alcohol for me," Jennie chimed in, followed by Clay's request for the spiked version.

Nick grinned. "All right, I'll meet you all on the verandah. I'll just need Grandma to allow me in the kitchen for a minute."

Nick joked with his grandmother about having a special pass based on his status in the family. Kathleen's endearing sense of humour shone through as she mimicked a gatekeeper sliding back the gates to allow him to enter.

As Nick prepared the drinks, the familiar scent of cinnamon and chocolate filled the air, stirring memories of family holidays. He smiled, taking Kathleen's advice to sprinkle dark chocolate shavings on top of the marshmallows, making the drinks extra special.

Maneuvering a tray of steaming cups through the doorways, Nick stepped onto the verandah where the rest were already seated near the heat lamps. "The ones with the marshmallows are for you and Mom, Em," he said, setting it down on the wicker table.

"You can stir it with the cinnamon stick if you like," Nick said to Emily, watching her eyes light up as she reached for her cup.

"We're so happy you can share Christmas with us, Emily.

Please make yourself at home; you're a part of the family now," Jennie said, raising her drink.

"Thank you, Jennie, that's so sweet. You sure know how to make someone feel welcome," Emily replied, smiling. "And I have to say—you people know how to turn a work project into a lot of fun."

Nick leaned back, feeling a wave of contentment. "We don't let chores get in the way of enjoying the simple pleasures."

Jennie nodded in agreement, smiling warmly at Emily. "Are you good at balancing work and play, Emily?"

Nick caught a brief hesitation in Emily's face. She was always so focussed, and so serious about her responsibilities. He waited, curious how she'd respond.

"I try," she replied with a light laugh. "But honestly," she said, raising her brows, "I could be better at balancing everything in my life."

Nick couldn't help but interject. "Em is one of those rare people who takes on everyone else's burdens, sometimes at her own expense. Not that I'm judging," he added quickly, "but I've seen it firsthand over these last four years."

Clay raised his spiked hot chocolate with a grin. "Well, you won't catch me doing that. Self-sacrifice isn't my thing."

Jennie chuckled along with him, and Nick smiled, thankful to be surrounded by the people he loved, especially with Emily sharing it all.

Chapter Three

Emily inhaled deeply as she and Nick headed toward the barn, the crisp sea air mingling with the earthy scents of pine and cedar, a sensory blend that stirred something peaceful in her. As they approached the open stable door, Emily quickened her step, eager to see Alexa's work. When she reached the stall, Emily saw Music standing there, majestic with her intricately braided mane gleaming under the soft light.

"Look, Nick!" Emily exclaimed, her voice filled with awe as she ran her fingers along the braided V's.

"This is a work of art." The braids were tied with red and white bands, and the rest of each section was left unbraided so that it looked like a waterfall of Music's blonde mane.

Nick grinned. "Yeah, Alexa's gotten pretty good at it over the years. Every Christmas we think she's outdone herself, and then the next year she tops it."

"And all this for the Open House on Friday?" Emily asked, marvelling at the detail.

"Yeah, it'll be a highlight for sure—along with whatever

Lexi decides to do with Music's tail. And then there's the pony cart," Nick added with a twinkle in his eye.

"What? Pony rides?" Emily asked, eyes widening. "And who'll drive the cart?"

"Stewart Owen, an old family friend. You might've seen him at the market on Saturday, but with the chaos that day, you probably didn't get a chance to meet him."

Emily smiled and looped her arms around Nick's neck, feeling a deep surge of warmth she hadn't expected. "I'm so glad you invited me here, Nick. I had no idea Christmas at Cliffhouse was this... magical. It's like a whole other world."

Nick pulled her closer, but she flexed back slightly to look into his eyes. "You kept this a secret, didn't you?" she teased with a lighthearted smile.

Nick laughed. "I just wanted to surprise you, that's all."

"Well, it's a wonderful surprise," Emily said, pressing her lips against his. For a moment, she closed her eyes and let herself feel the warmth, the love, and the sense of belonging she had been craving.

"Oh, pardon me," Jennie's voice chimed as she entered the stable. "Sorry to interrupt, but I just had to see what Alexa did with Music's mane."

"It's stunning," Emily said, still feeling the warmth of Nick's arms. "Just perfect."

Jennie beamed with pride. "Yes, and each year, it just gets better. Look at this French-braided forelock—that's new, and I hear it's quite the challenge."

As Jennie and Nick admired the braiding, Emily glanced back at Music, but her thoughts were on their kiss. Jennie had interrupted their embrace, but she hadn't interrupted the feeling blooming inside Emily, a feeling that Christmas here, with this family, meant something more. Jennie's earlier words reflected in her thoughts: *You're a part of the family now.*

For a fleeting moment, she wished she could hold on to this forever. But deep down, she knew her time here would end. Soon, she'd be back in England, far away from all this—the love, the warmth, the togetherness. How could she leave it all behind?

...

There always seemed to be plenty of food in the freezer for such times. With everyone busy getting ready for the Open House and all the other events around Christmas, even Kathleen didn't have time to prepare dinner that night. But she found time to thaw seven chicken pot pies and leave them warm in the oven so they could eat at their convenience.

As Nick helped Kyla and Alexa clean up the dishes, he caught glimpses of Emily, Clay, and Jennie settling around the living room fireplace. He watched for a moment—Emily nestled on the couch, her legs tucked beneath her, Jennie smiling gently as she sipped tea, and Clay leaning forward, gesturing as he spoke.

Drying the last dish, Nick wiped his hands on a towel and headed toward the living room. The soft crackle of the fire and the glow it cast across their faces made the room feel like its own little world, separate from the busyness of the kitchen. As he sank into a chair near the fire, the warmth from the flames wrapped around him, a familiar comfort after the busy day. Across from him, Emily tucked a blanket around her legs, her eyes glowing in the firelight. She looked peaceful and relaxed— a sight that filled Nick with contentment.

It had been a full day, but seeing Emily drawn into the fabric of his family so naturally made Nick feel like this was exactly where she belonged. He hadn't realized just how much he wanted her to feel at home here until tonight.

"Today was fun, wasn't it?" Nick said, leaning forward to poke at the fire, sending a spray of embers crackling up the chimney. "Is this what you imagined Christmas at Cliffhouse would be like Em?"

Emily nodded, her smile soft and warm. "Today was perfect. Your family is... wonderful. I had no idea Christmas at Cliffhouse would feel this special."

Nick grinned, stretching out his legs. "I guess we make a pretty big deal out of it."

"I can see that," she said, gazing at the fire. But something in her expression shifted—a flicker of something Nick couldn't quite place. *Worry? Or maybe just exhaustion from the day.*

He watched her for a second longer, his contentment tinted with an uneasiness he didn't understand. He was probably imagining it, yet he couldn't shake the feeling that something else was on Emily's mind.

Moving close to Emily, he bent down and whispered in her ear. "You okay?" he asked.

Emily's focus seemed to shift back to the present. "Yeah, I'm fine," she said, her smile returning. "Just thinking about a few things, that's all."

Nick felt a twinge of worry but pushed it aside. If something was bothering Emily, she would tell him... eventually. But for now, he wanted to savour these moments with his family and the love of his life.

"Well, if you need a real distraction, Em," Nick teased, "there's always more hot chocolate and marshmallows in the kitchen."

Emily chuckled, "You're dangerous with those marshmallows, you know."

Nick grinned, soaking in the cozy atmosphere. For now, everything felt right.

...

It was tempting to stay up late, but they all knew they had to be on their game to finish preparations for the Open House on Friday. Besides, Emily wanted to join Nick and his twin sisters at the community centre tomorrow. They would fill Christmas hampers for the needy and be present when the winners of the Christmas Bake-Off were announced.

Climbing the stairs with Nick, they walked down the hall to the last bedroom on the left, the creaky floorboards beneath their feet adding a familiar charm. She switched on the light, her eyes flicking to the bay window where the garland they'd hung draped gracefully. By the time they slipped under the eiderdown, it didn't take long for them to drift into a deep sleep.

The loud ding of Emily's phone jolted her awake. Always a light sleeper, she kept her phone by her bed for emergencies. Her heart sank as she saw her mother's name flash across the screen.

Not wanting to wake Nick, she threw back the covers and padded to the ensuite bathroom, gently closing the door behind her. "Mum, is everything okay?" she asked in a hushed voice, dread already creeping in.

Charlotte's voice came through, fragile and broken. "Emily, I don't know how much longer I can do this. Your father... he's getting worse. He spent all our Christmas savings, and I don't know what to do anymore."

Emily pressed a hand to her forehead, a wave of nausea rising as she tried to hold herself together. "What do you mean, Mum? How bad is it this time?"

"Fred disappeared again. Said he was going to a meeting, but I think he's using. He won't answer my calls." Charlotte paused before adding, "I'm scared, Em. I don't think I can face Christmas with him like this."

Emily's heart raced. She'd walked this path too many times before. When her father's heroin addiction spiraled out of control, she and her mother always felt helpless.

"I'm sorry, Mum. I wish I could be there to hug you so we could face this together. But, I can only send my love through the phone." She paused, trying to find the right words. "You know as well as I do, Mum... there's nothing we can do when he gets like this."

Emily heard the quiet sound of her mother's stifled sobs. It twisted her gut. "Could you stay with Aunt Lizzy for a bit, do you think?"

"I've already called her, love," Charlotte said, her voice wavering.

"Good. I know it's six months until I can come home, but my thoughts are always with you. I'm here, Mum, always."

Emily returned to bed, slipping in quietly beside Nick. She stared toward the ceiling, her mind racing, unable to shake the darkness that had come through the phone. Although her body ached for sleep, Emily tossed and turned without disturbing Nick, who remained blissfully unaware of the storm brewing in her life.

Chapter Four

Nick glanced at Emily, sound asleep, and figured she'd had a good night. She was a light sleeper, but island life so far seemed to help her rest better. Quietly getting up, he dressed in the bathroom, trying not to wake her.

In the kitchen, he greeted Kathleen with a warm hug. "Grandma, I see you're up and at 'em, as usual," Nick said.

"Well, today's the day I deliver my shortbread for judging," she replied.

"I can deliver it for you, Grandma, if Kyla will lend me her Forester. Em and I'll head into town around ten to help with the Christmas hampers."

"Thanks, Nick, but Jen and I will deliver them shortly. Judging starts at ten, and we will announce the winners at three o'clock today."

They both glanced up as Emily arrived in the kitchen, looking groggy, still in her pajamas. "Em, glad to see you're up, but you don't look at all rested. Is there something wrong?" Nick asked.

"No, not really," Emily said. "But Mum called after I'd fallen asleep, and I had trouble getting back to sleep again."

"Aw, yes, I know how that is," Kathleen said. "Your mind gets working overtime after something like that."

"Is she okay?" Nick persisted.

"It's Christmastime, that's all. She misses me," Emily said, shrugging her shoulders.

"Understandable," Nick said. "Coffee's on; shall I pour you a cup?"

"I hope it's extra strong," Emily joked. "What time do we leave for the community centre?"

* * *

The scents of cedar boughs and cinnamon greeted Emily and Nick as they stepped into the spacious room designated for filling Christmas hampers. The warmth of the room contrasted with the cool, crisp air outside. As volunteers bustled about, laughter and cheerful conversation filled the air.

Emily glanced around the room where rows of long wooden tables stretched across the large, open space, each one laden with colourful toys, neatly stacked cans, boxes of food, and handmade winter clothes. Plush toys—teddy bears and stuffed animals of every kind—sat in piles, waiting to be packed into hampers. Brightly coloured scarves, mittens, and hats, many knitted by the islanders themselves, created a vibrant contrast to the plain wooden tables.

"Look at this place," Emily said, her eyes lighting up. "Where do we start, Nick?"

"Maybe let's walk around a bit and see where everything is," he suggested, as they hung up their coats.

At the far end of the room, another row of tables held canned goods, boxed meals, and bags of rice, all sorted into neat stacks ready to be packed into family-sized hampers. Holly wreaths decorated every window, and Christmas lights twinkled around the frames, casting a warm, festive glow over the room. Sunlight streaming through the large windows along the east side of the room danced on red cellophane wrap and glittery stars, adding to the magic.

Emily noticed Nick eyeing the refreshment station set up near the entrance. "Shall we grab an apple cider or hot chocolate first?" she suggested. "You islanders sure know how to put on an event," she added, "even a so-called work project."

The room was alive with Christmas music playing in the background, the rustling of wrapping paper, and the hum of voices as people chatted, laughed, and worked together to pack the hampers.

Emily felt Nick's gentle nudge, his eyes crinkling at the corners, as he said, "Come on, let's see what we can help with."

They made their way to the table at the centre of the room, where a small group was organizing food hampers. "Nick! Emily!" Mrs. Kerrigan called out, beaming at them as they approached.

How does she know my name? Emily wondered.

The woman was elbow-deep in piles of donations, sorting cans and boxes of food with practiced efficiency. "I've got just the task for you two. How about packing these for the families with little ones?"

"Perfect," Nick said, already rolling up his sleeves.

Emily joined him, reaching for a plush teddy bear to tuck into a hamper. She glanced around, noting the effortless way everyone worked together. Islanders from all walks of life—young families, older couples, teenagers—came together for this annual tradition. It wasn't just about giving, it was about community, something Emily grew to love more than she ever thought possible.

"Here you go, dear," Mrs. Kerrigan said, handing her a stack of knitted scarves. "These are for the younger children, handmade by the women's knitting group. Aren't they sweet?"

"They're beautiful," Emily replied, tucking one into a hamper. "By the way," Emily asked Mrs. Kerrigan, "how did you know my name?"

"Oh, forgive me for not introducing myself," Mrs. Kerrigan said with a warm smile, "but everyone knows everyone's business here on the island—you'll find that out soon enough," she added unapologetically. "We've heard so much about Nick's special girl for the past four years, and we couldn't wait to meet you."

The words warmed Emily's heart, making her feel part of their lives even before they met. And Mrs. Kerrigan had a way about her that made Emily feel like she had known her for years. *Something like Nick's grandmother*, she mused.

As they worked, more islanders stopped by to chat. Mrs. Kerrigan's husband, Frank, paused to share a joke with Nick, while another couple offered them some homemade butter tarts. Emily felt included in the easy camaraderie. This wasn't her hometown, but it was beginning to feel like it. It seemed like the islanders had accepted her from the moment she'd arrived, not asking too many questions or making her feel like an outsider.

"You know," Nick said softly, leaning in, "everyone here thinks the world of you."

"But they don't even know me, Nick," she protested, her cheeks warming.

"It's true," he insisted, his voice full of affection. "You're making a difference here, Em. You're one of us now."

"Well, thanks for the compliment," Emily said, glancing at the floor. "But I think this is more about you than me," she claimed.

"What do you mean?" Nick asked, amused.

"They love you, not me, obviously," she teased. "And somehow, maybe by osmosis or something, I too am loved."

"Ah," Nick replied, "the old 'you're judged by the company you keep' kind of thing."

"Whatever," Emily said. "I'll take it, whatever it is. I wouldn't dream of arguing with this exceptionally lovely group of people... I just hope I can live up to the high bar they've set here."

Nick and Emily glanced up at the sound of giggles nearby. Children darted between the tables, laughing, as they tried to sneak away a toy or two, only to be redirected by their parents. The energy was infectious—bright, warm, and full of holiday cheer. Emily couldn't help but smile as she looked around. This wasn't about charity; it was the community coming together and sharing what they had with those who needed it most.

The hours passed quickly as Emily lost herself in the rhythm of the work. The laughter, the smiles, and the sheer generosity of everyone around her filled her with a sense of peace she hadn't expected. She was part of something bigger here, something that transcended her personal struggles.

...

Even though the awards presentation for the Christmas Bake-Off was only a room away, Nick and Emily barely made it on time. Three o'clock rolled around all too fast as they lost themselves in the joy of filling Christmas hampers.

Emily and Nick stepped into the hall, taking in the festive scene. Emily glanced at the long tables stretched along the walls, each one draped with tablecloths printed in cheerful candy cane stripes, adding to the festive charm. On top, a dazzling array of baked goods beckoned—gingerbread houses dripping with icing, trays of butter tarts glistening in the soft light, and elaborately decorated Christmas cakes perched like edible masterpieces. The scent of butter, vanilla, nutmeg, and cinnamon filled the air, blending with the hum of holiday chatter as visitors wandered from table to table, admiring the displays.

At the far end of the hall, a huge banner read, "Annual Sunrise Island Christmas Bake-Off." A small stage stood ready for the awards, with a cedar wreath decorating the podium. Around the stage, silver tinsel draped across the railings shimmered in the glow of fairy lights, adding an extra touch of festivity.

Rows of folding chairs filled the centre of the room, all facing the stage. A few clusters of people sat with their coats draped over the backs of their chairs, chatting amongst themselves and waving at passing friends. Some people stood near the edges, holding cups of hot drinks, their voices blending into the lively hum that filled the room.

Kathleen stood off to the side near the cookie section, smiling softly as she admired the rows of shortbread cookies entered by bakers of all ages. Her entry sat modestly on a ceramic plate decorated with tiny holly leaves, each cookie perfectly golden with a delicate sugar dusting. Other entries featured icing and decorations with tiny multi-coloured candies, red and green cherries, and small chocolate chips. Some resembled stained-glass windows with black lines separating the colours.

"Nick, you said that Kathleen always wins."

"Yes, Grandma's shortbread always wins," he said, with a playful grin. "You can almost see people placing bets on it."

"Do you think she's expecting to win again?" Emily asked.

"No, Grandma says she has no expectations. She doesn't enter for the prize—just for the joy of being part of the tradition... but the judging panel's different this year, so who knows what might happen."

Emily felt Nick's hand as he placed it on the small of her back, guiding her toward a pair of empty chairs near the middle. "Looks like the awards are about to start soon," he said, his voice low but filled with excitement. Emily nodded, still taking in the scene. Glancing toward the front of the room, she spotted Kathleen surrounded by well-wishers. The ease with which Kathleen navigated the crowd impressed her—modest and kind despite the inevitable praise. Emily couldn't help but feel at home here, surrounded by the festive atmosphere and the deep sense of community.

As they took their seats, the room buzzed with anticipation. More people were finding their way to the chairs, but a few lingered by the dessert displays, still savouring the last moments of judgment-free indulgence before the announcement of the winners. Children weaved through the crowd, tugging at their parents' sleeves, eager to see if their gingerbread houses had won.

The crowd quieted as the speaker, a local chef with silver hair and a Santa-like belly, stepped up to the podium, adjusting the microphone and tapping it twice to get the room's attention. Slowly, the voices hushed, and the final stragglers took their seats or stood in the back, waiting for the presentation to begin.

"It's wonderful to see such a fantastic turnout again this year. Thank you to all the bakers for bringing your incredible talent and holiday spirit to this event, and to everyone for making this Bake-Off such a special tradition."

After introducing the four judges, the speaker continued, starting with the winner of the butter tarts category. Emily watched the stage, her heart warming at the sense of community that filled the room, a reminder of why she had fallen in love with Sunrise Island.

"Now, let's move on to the shortbread cookies—always a crowd favourite!" he announced, his voice booming across the room. "This winning baker's cookies were a masterclass in simplicity and flavour. Flakey, buttery, and with just the right balance of sweetness." He paused for a moment, heightening the suspense. "The winner of this year's shortbread category is..."

Emily glanced at Kathleen. "Aw, she looks a bit nervous, don't you think, Nick? She's so humble; it's one of her most endearing traits."

Emily watched as heads turned in Kathleen's direction, some already nodding in expectation.

"And the first prize goes to... Kathleen Mitchell!"

A ripple of applause spread through the hall, accompanied by a few cheers. No one seemed particularly surprised, but Emily admired Kathleen as she placed a hand on her chest, her cheeks flushing. She exchanged a glance with Jennie, who stood beside her, grinning with pride.

Emily and Nick cheered as Kathleen walked to the stage, waving politely at a few familiar faces. She climbed the steps with the grace of someone used to the spotlight, yet she presented herself as though it were her first time up there.

"Thank you, everyone," she said, her voice warm and steady as she accepted the gold ribbon from the judge. "It's truly an honour. There were so many wonderful entries this year. I didn't expect to win again—I'm just happy to be here with all of you."

Tears glistened in Emily's eyes as she listened to Kathleen's gracious acceptance. The crowd clapped again, and a few people exchanged knowing smiles. Kathleen's humility was as legendary as her shortbread.

As Kathleen stepped down from the stage and walked back to Jennie's side, Emily noticed a new crowd gathering at the table featuring Kathleen's entry. *And I have the secret recipe,* Emily mused, filled with pride and appreciation for Nick's beloved grandmother and this fabulous tradition. *I'll never forget this day.*

Emily couldn't help but smile as people offered congratulations as Kathleen passed, and someone jokingly asked her for the secret to her recipe.

"Oh, just a little love," she said with a wink, though everyone knew her baking stemmed from decades of experience and meticulous attention to detail.

As the awards ceremony wound down, Emily, Nick, Kathleen, and Jennie mingled with others and laughed with old friends. Emily gave Kathleen a warm hug of congratulations, recognizing the ribbon in her hand served as a reminder of why Kathleen came back year after year—not for the prize, but for the community and the simple joy of sharing what she loved.

"Kathleen," Emily said, "your kindness in sharing your special recipe means all the more to me now, and I'll never forget it... your secret's safe with me."

As they said their goodbyes, Emily was deep in thought. Sunrise Island felt like a storybook at Christmastime, but today, it seemed especially magical. The twinkling lights seemed to reflect in Nick's eyes, and for a moment, Emily forgot all about the heavy decision weighing on her. Here, in this warm, buzzing room filled with laughter and holiday cheer, everything seemed possible.

Chapter Five

"Even your 'quick and easy' dinners are out-of-this-world, Grandma," Nick said, squeezing Kathleen. "And now, while Em and I clean up, how 'bout the rest of you set up for a game of charades?"

A chorus of agreement followed as the family moved toward the living room, happy chatter echoing through the cozy house. Rollo, their beloved German pointer, padded about the house, pausing for love wherever he found it. He'd hidden under the table during dinner, waiting for the inevitable piece of dropped food.

Nick caught Emily's eye as they gathered the plates, sensing something was slightly off. Even though she was smiling, there was a heaviness about her, something unsaid lingering between them.

They fell into a familiar rhythm, the soft clattering of dishes making conversation unnecessary. But Nick couldn't shake the feeling that Emily's mind was elsewhere, a stark contrast to her demeanour at the community centre. He wanted to ask what had changed, but now wasn't the time.

Instead, he squeezed her hand as they finished cleaning, hoping his gesture said what words could not.

The living room had been transformed by the time they found the others. They pushed the coffee table out of the way and rearranged the seating, so each team had a view of the player acting out the charade.

"You two are on Clay's team," Kathleen announced to Nick and Emily. "And Jen, Kye, and Lexi are on the other team. I'm going to sit in my favourite chair and watch the fun for a while, but I'll be heading to bed early," she said, yawning. "It's been a long day."

"I'll go first," Nick volunteered, grinning as he reached into a bowl filled with slips of paper. "

Alexa turned over the timer and Nick went into action, holding up three fingers, followed by two. Using his hand to make waves, he frowned when Emily shouted "waves", "ocean", and "sea" in quick succession. Nick then mimicked grasping a steering wheel, and Clay shouted "boat". Nick nodded, using his fingers to show he was now on the third word of the phrase. He stiffened his arms and made a marching gesture. "march", shouted Emily.

"Soldier", "army", shouted Clay.

"Parade", shouted Emily, guessing the third word correctly.

"Lighted boat parade" shouted Clay, winning the round just ahead of the one-minute deadline. The three cheered triumphantly, high-fiving each other as Jennie chose a slip of paper from the bowl.

The game was in full swing, the room filled with laughter and wild guesses as each person took their turn acting out Christmas-themed charades. Nick was enjoying the moment, the warmth of family around him, but his attention kept shifting to Emily. She laughed at all the right moments, her eyes crinkling in that way he loved, but he couldn't shake the feeling that part of her was elsewhere.

Just as Emily stood to take her turn, her phone buzzed. Nick saw the change in her immediately—her hand clenched around her phone, her face draining of colour as she peered at the display screen. She forced a smile at Nick, but her eyes told a different story, one filled with worry and something deeper—fear, maybe? Guilt? Nick couldn't quite place it.

She pulled Nick aside, her voice low. "I need a moment; it's Mum."

Nick's stomach tightened. He calculated it was around four in the morning in England, so he decided not to suggest that Em call her back later. *It could be urgent.*

"No worries, Em. I can take your turn," he said, as Emily headed toward the verandah, grabbing her coat off its hook in the hall. Rollo followed her out the door and disappeared from view as Emily shut the door behind them.

"I think it's her mum," Nick said quietly, trying to keep his tone light, though the worry gnawed at him. "Lottie probably just misses her," he added, hoping it was that simple.

"Lottie," Jennie said, "such a cute name."

"Short for Charlotte," Nick explained. "I think it's a popular name in England."

Nick went through the motions, acting out his charade and laughing along with the others, but part of him was elsewhere— outside, on the verandah, with Emily. He hung on for another round but, when Emily still hadn't returned, he headed out to the verandah.

"Is everything okay, Em?" Nick asked as Emily set her phone down. He saw the tension in her eyes, even though she tried to force a smile.

"It's nothing, just some stuff with my family. I'll sort it out," Emily said, brushing him off with a wave of her hand.

Nick did not look convinced as he opened the screen door, and then the main door, Rollo nosing in ahead of both of them.

In the living room, Jennie asked, "How's your mum doing, Emily?"

When Jennie asked about her mother, Emily hesitated. It was just for a second, but Nick noticed—the slight falter in her voice, the way her fingers fiddled with the edge of her sleeve.

"She's okay, Jennie; thanks for asking," Emily said, her words careful, measured. "It's Christmastime, that's all, and the first time I haven't been home for the holidays."

"I can imagine that's tough," Jennie replied, smiling. Maybe Nick'll be with you next Christmas and I'll be the one phoning him," she chuckled.

Nick watched Emily closely, the laughter of the game barely registering in his mind. He hated feeling kept out of reach like Emily had built a wall between them, one he could not climb no matter how hard he tried.

...

In the soft glow of the bedroom light, Emily and Nick got ready for bed. Glancing around the room, Emily said, "Oh, I must have left my phone downstairs, Nick. I'll be right back."

Walking downstairs, Emily noticed the lights were still on in the kitchen and living room. Hearing a clatter in the kitchen, she entered the room and saw Jennie stirring something in a glass.

"Oh, you're still up," she remarked, wondering what Jennie was preparing.

"Yes," Jennie said, "I'm having apple cider vinegar in water." She raised the glass to her lips and gulped the contents. Jennie grimaced. "Ooof, it's pretty awful, but it does the trick for my acid reflux. As much as I love Mom's breaded chicken, I end up paying for it overnight," she said with a chuckle.

"I'm glad you found something that works," Emily said, standing at the edge of the kitchen, her fingers pressing into the edge of the doorframe. "I think I left my phone down here—probably in the living room."

"Oh, I'm good at finding things. Let me help you look," Jennie said, following her just as Emily spotted her phone on the fireplace mantel.

"Got it," she said, turning to Jennie as she reached for the phone and looked at the screen, hoping there wasn't a missed message.

"We can't be without our phones, as much as we'd like sometimes," Jennie mused.

"True," Emily said, "and as much as I'd like to shut the ringer off at night, I can't do that to Mum."

Jennie stayed quiet for a moment before sinking into the sofa. "Sit for a bit, will you, Emily? I know it's late, but we don't get many chances to chat, just ourselves."

"No, it's like a beehive around here, as far as I can see," Emily laughed softly, drawn to Jennie's warmth.

"I was just wondering about something, if you don't mind my asking," Jennie began.

Emily couldn't help but feel nervous, not wanting to explain things she may not be sure about. Her fingers twisted the ring on her hand, a habit she hadn't been able to shake since she'd decided to return to England.

"So, you're returning to England after graduation in June... to live permanently—is that right, dear?" Jennie settled into the sofa, her quiet patience giving Emily the space she needed to speak.

"Yes," Emily said, not feeling pressured to answer. Throughout the years Emily dated Nick, he'd painted his mother as nurturing and non-judgemental—just the qualities Emily needed right now.

"And how wonderful you can set up practice with a group of your friends," Jennie added with a smile. When Emily didn't reply right away, Jennie continued. "And you know, I'm sure, that Nick told you he's always dreamed of practicing on the island. I'm pretty sure he has his eye on a space in the diversified clinic in Grace Square... where Alexa lives."

"I know," Emily said. Sighing deeply, she glanced at the dying embers in the fireplace, her shoulders slumped.

"Look," she said, her voice barely above a whisper. "That's not the reason I'm returning to England. The truth is... Mum needs me more than anyone knows."

"So, it's not just that she misses you, then?"

Emily stared at her hands, unable to meet Jennie's eyes. "Jennie, I want to tell you something I haven't even told Nick." The words felt like a betrayal, but Jennie had a way of listening that felt like permission—permission to be honest, to let the walls down.

"It's my dad," Emily said, her throat tightening. "He's... addicted to heroin."

The words came out brittle like they could shatter if she said them too loud. Emily's heart pounded, a familiar wave of shame washing over her. She dropped her gaze again, not wanting to see pity in Jennie's eyes. She couldn't handle that.

"My mum... she's been coping with this since I was young. And I think she's at the breaking point right now with me not being home for Christmas."

"That's why you're going back to England in June. It's not just about your friend's clinic, is it?" Jennie asked softly.

"Mum needs me," Emily replied. "To leave my mother to cope with my dad by herself, well, it's just unconscionable. I cannot do it."

Emily swallowed hard, finally lifting her gaze to meet Jennie's. She expected to see concern, or worse, disappointment. But all she saw was kindness. Understanding. The knot in her stomach loosened just a little.

Emily held her breath, waiting for Jennie's response, half-expecting her to suggest that Nick deserved to know. Instead, Jennie reached across the sofa and placed a warm hand on hers, the simple gesture grounding her.

"That's an awful lot for you to carry around. But now I understand why you've been preoccupied, Emily." Jennie said with a smile. "I don't want to pry, dear, but is there a reason you haven't let Nick know about this? I mean, he talks as if you're staying."

"I'm sure it sounds stupid," Emily said, "but I thought he'd see me differently if he knew, and I just couldn't risk it. And, knowing that I'd have to move back home and break his heart, I thought it would be easier on both of us if he knew I had an amazing job offer instead."

"I understand," Jennie whispered. "And I won't say anything to Nick. This is yours to share when you're ready."

Emily's eyes burned with tears she hadn't expected. She blinked quickly, trying to keep them at bay, but one slipped free, trailing down her cheek.

Jennie didn't push; she didn't try to offer hollow reassurances. Instead, she simply held Emily's hand, and that was enough.

"I love Nick," Emily whispered, her voice trembling. "But I can't... I can't do this to him. Not yet. I'm scared it'll be too much for him."

It wasn't Nick's fault—he'd always been there for her. But this... this was different. The weight of her father's addiction and her mother's silent suffering were burdens too heavy to share with anyone else right now.

"I just need time," Emily said, her voice thick with emotion. Please, don't tell him. Let me figure out how to do it."

Jennie's fingers squeezed hers gently. "I won't say a word."

Relief washed over Emily, and for the first time since she had come to Canada four years ago, Emily felt like she wasn't carrying this alone. Jennie understood more than expected—it was exactly what she needed.

"Thank you," Emily whispered, squeezing Jennie's hand. She wiped at her tears quickly, a quiet resolve settling over her. She wasn't ready to face Nick with this yet, but maybe she could get there.

"I know my son. He'll love you no matter what."

Emily bit her lower lip. "I guess I've been foolish."

"Not at all, dear," Jennie said, lifting her hand from Emily's. "That's a heavy burden to carry, Emily. No wonder you feel torn."

Emily began to feel better, relieved to finally share her story with Jennie.

"And you're not alone, not by a long shot." Jennie continued. "Right here on Sunrise, I know several people who've gone through something similar... including Bev, my best friend."

Emily looked into Jennie's eyes, smiling. "Oh," she chuckled, "even your storybook island has its troubles."

"Everywhere has its troubles," Jennie replied, raising her brows. "But listen," she said, standing up, "we'd better get to bed. Patrick arrives tomorrow, and we have only two days left 'til the Open House."

"I'm excited to meet Clay's son," Emily said, happy about the change of topic, yet grateful that Jennie seemed unphased by her story. They hugged each other goodnight, switched off the lights, and headed upstairs. The steady thump of Rollo's tail against his dog bed was a comforting rhythm in the quiet house.

...

The morning sun filtered through the kitchen window, casting a warm glow over the bustling scene. Emily stood by the counter, watching Kathleen, her apron dusted with flour, kneading dough for a homemade loaf of bread. "I think Patrick might like this cinnamon-raisin loaf, don't you, Emily?"

"Who wouldn't like a homemade loaf of anything, Kathleen?" Emily said with a smile. The scent of yeast and cinnamon enveloped her, and she imagined how pleased Patrick would be to have a cup of the Sunrise Island coffee they'd placed in his kitchen, along with a freshly toasted slice of Kathleen's homemade bread. The holiday scents comforted Emily and made her long for home, yet her heart ached at the thought of leaving.

"Em, "Alexa said, her eyes bright with excitement. "Want to come with Kye and me? We're decorating Patrick's place to make his welcome extra special."

"Yeah, I'd love to," Emily said, following Alexa out the kitchen door.

Kyla was already unpacking their surprises, beaming widely as the others entered the little house beside hers. They busied themselves, laughing and chatting as they added thoughtful touches of the island throughout the cottage—Sunrise Island coffee, fresh flowers from their greenhouse, and local chocolates thoughtfully arranged on one of Jennie's clay dishes. They stocked the fridge with a few staples so Patrick wouldn't need to shop as soon as he landed. The thought of him walking into that cozy space, surrounded by their personal touches, made Emily smile.

"Don't forget the welcome sign," Alexa called out, glancing at Emily with a twinkle in her eye. "Patrick's going to need to know he's part of the family now."

"Got it!" Emily replied, feeling gratitude for the family that had made her feel the same way—a near stranger welcomed with open arms. Moments like these left her torn. The love she felt for them only made her decision to return to England more difficult.

Kyla popped her head into the kitchen from the porch, her cheeks flushed with excitement. "Emily, can you help me hang the lights on the porch?"

"Absolutely!" Emily replied, a smile spreading across her face. But first, she set the welcome sign in the front window and stepped back to admire it once outside. "Perfect," she murmured to herself, feeling a surge of warmth at how inviting it looked.

Kyla handed her a length of twinkling lights, and together, they draped the strands across the porch, adding a sprinkle of cheer to the crisp winter air.

"Let me get that last bit," Emily said to Kyla. "I don't want you to fall, that's for sure," she said, smiling. "When's your baby due?"

"Not until July," Kyla said. "I'm not nauseous anymore, so that's something else to celebrate," she said with a laugh.

Once they finished hanging the twinkling lights, Emily returned to the kitchen to see if Kathleen's loaf was ready.

"Just in time," Kathleen said as she sliced the golden loaf, its aroma filling the room. "Here, dear, try a piece."

Emily accepted a slice, the warm, pillowy bread almost melting in her hands. As she sank her teeth into the slice, the rich, buttery flavors enveloped her senses, each bite a comforting delight. She closed her eyes, savoring the simple pleasure of homemade goodness.

"You know how to make someone feel welcome," she said with genuine admiration.

Kathleen smiled softly. "We want Patrick to feel at home.

Everyone needs a little kindness, especially during the holidays."

As the family prepared for Patrick's arrival, Emily couldn't help but feel a sense of belonging that she hadn't experienced in a long time. She glanced at the cozy house with its twinkling lights and welcome sign, envisioning Patrick stepping through the door and feeling the warmth of their hospitality.

As the days ticked by, a question lingered in Emily's heart: *How can I walk away from this?*

...

After lunch, Emily arranged a garland of pine and berries along the dining room table. She glanced up as Alexa came out of the home office carrying a cardboard box.

"I'm going to braid Music's tail... want to watch?" Alexa asked.

"I'd love to, Lexi," Emily replied. "I'll join you as soon as I'm done here, okay?"

As Alexa headed out the kitchen door toward the barn, Emily was about to pack up the remaining decorations when her phone rang. Her heart sank. *I might as well be back in England.*

Giving herself an attitude check before answering her phone, she smiled. "Hi, Mum. How are things today?" Emily could hear Lottie crying on the other end of the phone.

"Em," she said, "he hasn't come home yet. I'm scared something's happened to him."

Emily stood, gripping the phone tightly. She felt numb, unsure of what to say.

Charlotte broke the silence. "I'm sorry, sweetheart. I didn't want to interrupt your Christmas, but... I don't know where else to turn."

The sound of her mother's tears broke Emily's heart.

"Mum, please try to hang on. He's done this many times before, and he always comes home, eventually. Please try not to worry."

When Lottie didn't respond, Emily continued, "Even if I were back home with you, Mum, what could I do—report him missing? It hasn't been long enough for that. All you can do right now is ask if anyone's seen him."

Charlotte sighed, her voice filled with weariness. "I know, love. It's hard not knowing where he is, especially during the holidays."

"Of course, Mum. Please try to do something nice for yourself. It is Christmas, after all." Nestled in the warmth of Cliffhouse, Emily couldn't shake the guilt of enjoying Christmas while her mother faced it alone.

As Emily hung up, she felt the weight of the conversation steal her enthusiasm for the festivities at Cliffhouse. *I can't keep this from Nick much longer. I can't keep pretending that everything's fine.*

...

Everyone gathered on the verandah in their winter coats, heat lamps blazing and hurricane lamps casting a warm glow. With steaming cups in hand and Christmas music playing softly in the background, the air was thick with anticipation of Patrick's arrival.

As Clay's SUV crunched up the gravel driveway, excitement spilled out from the verandah. Everyone waved and shouted greetings, while Rollo wagged his tail so hard his whole back end swayed. Emily felt Nick wrap his arm around her as she joined in the others' excitement, despite not having met Patrick yet.

Emily stepped back as Clay helped him unload his luggage, watching as Patrick greeted everyone with hugs, his expression bright and cheerful. He flashed a big smile when she introduced herself and offered a warm handshake.

"I've heard so many wonderful things about you, Emily. It's a pleasure to meet you."

At that moment, Emily's worries about her latest call from her mother seemed to dissolve. But as the initial excitement settled, she found herself alone with her thoughts again.

...

"Care for another piece of cake, Patrick?" Kathleen asked as they gathered for after-dinner snacks.

Emily settled into a chair near the fire, sipping a glass of blackberry dessert wine from the Sunrise Island winery. She struggled to hide her distress, forcing a brave smile as Nick laughed and chatted with his sisters and Patrick at the table. She felt herself slipping away from the conversation, an observer rather than a participant.

"Did you hear from your mum today, Em?" Jennie asked quietly, having noticed Emily retreat into her thoughts.

"Um hmm," Emily replied, hoping Jennie wouldn't delve deeper.

"Yes, you seem a little down. Just let me know if you want to talk, okay?" Jennie offered, with concern in her eyes.

"I'm okay, Jennie," Emily said, smiling slightly. She glanced at Nick, not wanting to dampen his cheerful mood. But a flicker of worry crossed her mind—*what if Jennie intervened and told Nick the truth?* Emily planned to let him know when she was ready.

Chapter Six

At the Christmas market, the day after Nick and Emily arrived at Cliffhouse for the holiday, Nick had discreetly met with Joshua, the local jeweler who had a table set up. This was the perfect opportunity for Nick to slip away while Jennie and Bev got to know Emily.

Having noticed Emily's ring on the dresser in their bedroom, he had carefully placed it on a piece of paper and traced its circumference before returning it to its original spot.

"Can you use this diagram to size an engagement ring for me?" Nick asked Joshua, shoving the paper his way.

"Sure thing," Joshua replied, glancing at the drawing. "What do you have in mind?"

Nick checked to make sure Emily wasn't watching, then slid his hand into the inside pocket of his coat, pulling out a worn ring box. "I don't want Emily to see this," he cautioned. "Maybe you could turn your back to her... she's over by the food stand."

He watched as Joshua turned away and opened the box, revealing his great-grandmother's diamond ring nestled inside.

"Hmm, this is an antique," he said, tilting the box to inspect the ring. "I'd say it's from before 1920—maybe 1918—and it has a platinum band."

"Yes, that sounds about right," Nick replied. "Mom mentioned that date. After it's resized, can you clean the ring and tighten the claws?"

"My pleasure, Nick. I rarely see a gorgeous antique like this. But don't worry... I'll treat it with care. I can have it ready by Monday at noon."

On Monday, while Nick and Emily strolled along Sea Star Beach, he'd seized another opportunity to slip away while she shopped for a Christmas decoration for their room.

In the jewellery shop, Nick opened the lid of a new velvet ring box, a smile lighting up his face at the sight of the dazzling ring. "I think she'll love this. She's into vintage things—like our old farmhouse. Truth be told, I think Em's a good old-fashioned girl underneath it all."

"The best kind," Joshua said. "I'm not a fan of Botox and false eyelashes."

Nick chuckled. "Yeah, feels like a masquerade sometimes, doesn't it? But if it makes them feel better about themselves, then what's the harm?"

Joshua nodded thoughtfully. "Can't argue with that."

As they discussed the nature of beauty, an image of Emily flashed in Nick's mind—her blonde hair in perfect French braids. *She's a natural beauty*, he mused, but a deeper thought crept in. *But is there more to Emily than meets the eye?*

Saying goodbye to Joshua, Nick headed toward the Christmas shop, his great-grandmother's ring safely tucked away in his pocket.

...

With only three more days until Christmas Eve, when Nick planned to propose to Emily, he locked the bedroom door and again checked the hiding place for the ring. He had loosened two stitches in the bottom hem of the bedroom drapes to fit the box inside. Running his fingers along the top of the hem, he found the opening and withdrew the ring box. As he opened the lid, his eyes lit up just as they had the last time. *It's exquisite, just like Em. I'm a very lucky man.*

...

Jennie heard Clay shout to his son as he hauled an A-frame ladder toward the tall fir tree in the centre of their circular driveway. "We don't want to put you to work on your first day here, Patrick."

"I don't feel right if I'm not doing something constructive," he joked, a playful grin on his face.

"Good to hear! We could use all the help we can get for the Open House in two days," Clay replied, positioning another ladder against the tree.

Kyla emerged from the house, her arms full of colourful decorations.

"You're just in time, Patrick! We have enough ornaments to decorate a small village. Think you can handle it?"

"Absolutely! Just point me in the right direction," he said, stepping forward to help.

Jennie arranged tables and chairs on the patio as they started hanging ornaments. She glanced back at the tree adorned with twinkling lights and vibrant baubles. The atmosphere felt festive, laughter echoing around her, and she couldn't help but smile.

"Hey, Jennie! Do you think we should use the gold ribbons or the silver?" Kyla called out, holding up two spools.

"Gold! It'll add a warm touch," Jennie replied, anticipating the gathering.

Patrick climbed the ladder, carefully hanging an ornament near the top. "This tree is going to look amazing!" he exclaimed, his enthusiasm infectious.

"Just wait until we turn the lights on!" Clay added, stepping back to admire their progress. "We'll have to test them first to make sure they all light up," he said, heading toward the house.

Emily took a moment to breathe in the festive air, watching the family work together. It stood in stark contrast to the turmoil she had been feeling, but for the first time in days, she felt a sense of peace.

With a playful nudge, Kyla called up to Patrick, "Make sure you don't fall! We need you for the party, not just for decorating!"

"I've worked as a roofer, so I've got this," Patrick replied, laughter in his voice.

As the sun set, casting its warmth over the preparations, Jennie couldn't shake the feeling that this Open House would be special. It was more than just an event; it was a celebration of family, love, and new beginnings—especially for Patrick.

And dare she also hope for a new beginning for Nick and Emily? When Nick had called before leaving Toronto, asking her to set aside his great-grandmother's ring so he could have it resized, Jennie knew he was dead serious about Emily. But now, aware of Emily's real reason for returning to England in June, she felt on edge. Torn between her loyalty to her son and her understanding of Emily's plight, she was worried sick.

She didn't want to pry and ask Nick when he planned to propose, but she figured it had to be soon. Yet, she now knew that Emily was already juggling more than she could handle with her parents' issues looming over her.

As Patrick adjusted an ornament on the tree, Jennie caught his eye and smiled. He seemed to bring a fresh energy to the family, and she dared to hope it wasn't just wishful thinking. This holiday felt different—filled with the promise of healing for them all. She wanted Nick and Emily to find their way together, facing the challenges ahead with love and understanding. Maybe the spirit of the season would help them forge a new beginning and light the way forward.

Chapter Seven

"What time do we leave for the lighted boat parade, Nick?" Emily asked.

"Probably around seven," Nick replied. "If you need a warmer coat, I have an extra."

"No thanks; I'll dress in layers. And, if it's alright with you, maybe we could bring this wool blanket," she said, flipping over a corner to check the label. "Made right here on the island, of course," she chuckled. "I think I'll buy one for Mum and save it 'til next Christmas when she can appreciate it more."

I hope we can all spend Christmas together next year," Nick said. "We'd love to meet your parents."

"They'd adore your family, Nick; anyone would. But it's unlikely they could afford to travel this far," Emily said as she rolled up the wool blanket and stuffed it into her backpack. "And on a different topic... Your grandmother invited me to help make fudge... want to join?"

"Ah, no, I'll leave the cooking to you two," Nick said, laughing. "But I can do a taste test if you like," he offered.

"We have our own tastebuds, thanks, Nick," Emily joked.

"Fine," Nick replied. "I'll check in with Stewart Owen to confirm everything's set for the pony rides tomorrow. I'll see you at dinnertime, okay?"

He leaned in for a quick kiss, stepping back to admire her. Sweeping a hand through her blonde hair, he looked into her eyes and said, "I'm crazy about you, babe."

"Love you too," Emily replied, kissing his cheek before heading down to the kitchen.

...

"Maple fudge and chocolate marshmallow," Kathleen said, answering Emily's question about the flavours of the day as they stood in the cozy kitchen. The rich, caramel-like sweetness of warm maple syrup filled the air with a comforting and inviting fragrance.

"Ah, yes, that's Canadian maple syrup, I bet," Emily replied, grinning.

"You know it," Kathleen beamed. "And I only use dark syrup for the best flavour. We'll have to send some home with you. We make it right here on the farm, you know."

"Ha, why am I not surprised?" Emily said, recalling the exquisite taste of Kathleen's famous apple pancakes smothered in maple syrup. She imagined her mother savouring that treat, a hint of longing in her heart.

"Now, let's get started on another batch," Kathleen said, pulling out a heavy saucepan and measuring cups. "Fudge can be tricky, but I'll show you a few tricks to get it just right."

Emily stepped close, her curiosity piqued. "I've always had trouble getting the consistency right. It either hardens too much or not enough."

Kathleen nodded knowingly. "Many people struggle with

that. It's all about the temperature and timing. You must watch it closely. Here, let me show you."

As Kathleen poured the sugar, milk, maple syrup, and corn syrup into the saucepan, she talked Emily through each step, her voice warm and encouraging. "The key is to bring it to a gentle boil and stir constantly. If it bubbles too hard, it'll cook too fast."

Emily leaned in, trying to absorb every word, but her mind wandered back to her father. She thought about her mother's last call, the weight of her father's addiction pressing heavily in her heart. How could she return to England in June, knowing what awaited her?

"Are you alright, dear?" Kathleen asked gently, sensing the shift in Emily's demeanor. "You seem a bit preoccupied."

"Oh, it's nothing," Emily replied, forcing a smile. "Just thinking about... home, that's all."

Kathleen continued stirring, her voice warm. "It can be tough leaving family behind, especially during the holidays. But you know you're always welcome here. This is your home, too."

"Those words mean so much, Kathleen," Emily said, yearning to share her secret with Nick's grandmother. She was sure Kathleen would respond with the same warmth as Jennie, yet fear and uncertainty tangled in her mind, chipping away at her courage.

Kathleen continued, her voice bringing Emily back to the moment. "Ready to give it a try?" she asked, her eyes crinkling with a warm smile as she handed Emily a wooden spoon.

"Absolutely!" Emily replied, taking the spoon with renewed determination. For now, she would focus on getting the fudge just right—and leave her worries outside Kathleen's kitchen.

"Now, once we reach the soft ball stage—about 238 degrees —let it cook undisturbed. Patience is key," Kathleen instructed.

Emily nodded, grateful for both the distraction and Kathleen's comforting presence. As they stirred the mixture together, a quiet hope began to settle within her that she'd somehow find a way to balance her love for Nick with the pull of her family's struggles. *But that would be a Christmas miracle.*

"Yes, it's chilly," Nick said, pulling a wool toque over his head, "but the sky is clear. The sail-past is weather dependent, Em, and I didn't want you to have to wait 'til next year if it rained."

A pang of sadness washed over Emily as she heard the hope in Nick's voice, believing they would spend Christmas together next year.

He doesn't seem to get it, but that's my fault. She offered him a small smile, but inside, her mind spun. *How can I keep pretending this isn't tearing me apart?*

Hundreds of spectators had already gathered when the Mitchell family found parking spots near Ganges Harbour. Jennie, Clay, Patrick, and Kathleen stepped out of Jennie's white Audi, while Nick, Emily, Kyla, and Alexa climbed out of Kyla's Forester. Together, they found a perfect spot along the shoreline, just beyond the paved walkway and away from the busy dock. A blazing bonfire illuminated the faces of the onlookers, who huddled close, soaking up its warmth.

"Ah," Nick said to Emily, turning away from the water as

live music floated over from the Treehouse Café. "That's the same quartet we heard last Monday when we popped in for a quick bite. Remember, Em?" He wrapped a wool blanket gently around her shoulders, but it barely seemed to register. Nick followed her gaze to the crowd of young families hurrying toward a tugboat that had just docked. Among the lighted reindeer, elves, candy canes, and wrapped gifts, Santa appeared on the bow, a bulging bag slung over his shoulder. Excited children wearing neon plastic jewelry crowded together, barely leaving space for Santa to disembark the boat, their eyes fixed on the spectacle.

"He has treats for everyone, Em, and that means us, too."

"Aw, that's so sweet, Nick, but let's leave it for the others. I have had enough treats at Cliffhouse to last me a lifetime."

"I get it, Em, and I hate to tell you this... but it's only just beginning."

"Oh, no," Emily joked, "I'll arrive back in England twenty pounds heavier, and they won't even recognize me."

As a sailboat adorned with twinkling lights glided across the water, Nick smiled, his heart lifting as Emily's eyes sparkled with wonder. Strings of multicolored lights spiraled up the mast and cascaded down like a waterfall, draping the hull in a festive glow. The lights danced on the rippling water, amplifying the scene's magic.

"That's magnificent," Emily breathed, as the familiar tune of *"The Twelve Days of Christmas"* floated across the harbour.

"Look at that one," Nick said, pointing to a wooden boat with a command bridge and a neon orca wearing a Santa hat featured on the side.

Vessels of all sizes—powered by engines, propelled by sails, and moved by the strength of people—sailed across the harbour.

"There were 26 entries this year," Nick said proudly, and there are prizes for the top decorated, the most impressive all-around crew, and I'm not sure what else. But, as you can see, Em, this isn't just a stunning display of decorated ships..."

"I know, babe. It is yet another example of the island's community spirit."

Nick caught a hint of wistfulness in Emily's eyes and her smile seemed forced.

"Yep, it's a cherished tradition here, that's for sure," he added.

"A twinkling tradition of Christmas shippers," Emily quipped, but Nick wasn't fooled. The spark of joy in her eyes quickly faded, overshadowed by her familiar cloud of worry.

He laughed at her corny joke, trying to hold on to the moment.

"Now I'm craving a candy cane, Em," he said, pointing at a tugboat adorned with two giant candy canes on the forward deck and a family of snowmen on the upper. "I bet Santa has two in his sack with our names on them."

As Emily looked in the direction of the tugboat, Nick opened his thermos. He took a swig of hot cider as his eyes swept over the lighted restaurants and festive decorations around the harbour. Caught up in the moment, he leaned in to kiss Emily, but his heart sank when her phone rang.

Not again. He didn't even have to guess—it was probably Lottie, just like the other times.

"I can't ignore her, Nick. I promised her I would call her back."

Without a word, Emily turned away, walking down the path and out of earshot. Nick watched her go, his stomach tightening with every step she took. Standing alone, he stared at the festive lights around him, but they felt distant now. *She's slipping away, and I'm damned if I know how to get her back.*

When Emily finally returned, her face was pale, her body tense. Nick couldn't hold it in any longer.

"I feel like we're on a roller coaster, Em. One minute, you're this carefree, fun-loving woman, and the next, it's like you're carrying the weight of the world."

Emily's eyes filled with tears, and she swallowed hard. "I know, honey, and I'm sorry. But I can't help it. I love my mum so much—I'm her only child, remember..."

Nick exhaled sharply, his voice softening. "Well, I get the part about loving someone so much you can't bear to be without them."

Chapter Nine

With just a few hours until the Mitchell family's traditional Open House, Cliffhouse was buzzing with last-minute preparations. Jennie glanced at her mother, who was double-checking the food for what had to be the third time that morning.

"Mom, everything looks fabulous," Jennie said, placing her hand on Kathleen's arm. "Why don't you take a break? You have already done so much. I want you to relax and enjoy the celebration tonight."

Kathleen hesitated for a moment, then nodded. "Maybe you're right, Jen. There's nothing more I can do here, and I want to enjoy every minute."

As Kathleen left the kitchen, Jennie opened the fridge and smiled at the sight of it jam-packed with food. It was overflowing with her mother's efforts, a testament to Kathleen's love for tradition and family. Jennie lifted the freezer lid, pulling out a few items to thaw for the inevitable early arrivals.

Outside, someone had moved the verandah furniture aside

to create a cozy seating area with heat lamps, where guests could gather to enjoy the warmth while taking in the festivities from a higher vantage point.

Meanwhile, Patrick, Nick, and Clay had just unloaded the wooden dance floor from a rented truck, positioning it on the far side of the driveway. Anti-slip strips would protect dancers from falling should frost set in. The travelling musicians would arrive in their truck and transform the box into a makeshift stage, just like they had done in previous years.

"Oh, I see you haven't forgotten the key ingredient, Lexi," Jennie teased as Alexa strolled onto the verandah, holding a fresh sprig of mistletoe.

"Of course not, Mom," Alexa replied, grinning. "Don't forget—I'm bringing the esteemed Dr. Kevin Hunter to the gathering tonight," she added, her eyes sparkling.

"Esteemed for what?" Jennie asked, playing along.

"Um, that remains to be seen," Alexa joked. "As long as he doesn't hold *himself* in high esteem, we'll be just fine."

Jennie scanned the rafters and the posts lining the verandah. "What about up here?" she suggested, pointing to the apex of the ceiling. "There'll be an open area in the center of the room where unsuspecting couples might find themselves standing under the mistletoe without even realizing it," she added with a laugh. "That'll be fun!"

"That's probably the only sensible spot, Mom," Alexa said. "I thought the same. We'll have to drop it down, or no one will see it."

"I may have some sparkly ribbon left over if you want," Jennie suggested.

"That'll make it stand out," Alexa said, smiling brightly.

"By the way, dear, what does it even mean... kissing beneath the mistletoe?" Jennie asked.

"I don't know, Mom. It adds a kind of *Je ne sais quoi*, Kyla said, shrugging her shoulders. "I googled it on my phone and got all kinds of answers. Many people see it as a symbol of love and romance, fertility and life, peace and goodwill... but mostly, it's pretty and fun, so I'm all for it."

Jennie chuckled. "Well, all I know is that the berries and leaves are poisonous, so we'd better keep an eye on Rollo." With that, Jennie headed into the house, on a mission to find the sparkly ribbon.

As Jennie emerged from the home office, a scant spool of ribbon in hand, she felt thirsty and headed into the kitchen first. Standing at the faucet with glass in hand, movement outside caught her eye. In the breezeway between Kyla's cottage and the farmhouse, Kyla and Emily stretched out on yoga mats, facing the sea, oblivious to the goings-on behind them. It warmed Jennie's heart to see the closeness developing between Emily and the rest of the family.

As Jennie gulped a full glass of water, Alexa appeared at the kitchen entrance. "Where did you have to go to get the ribbon, Mom... the village?"

"Ha, sorry, dear. We all need to keep up our hydration, especially now. Drinking too much coffee and wine alone can deplete us," Jennie reminded Alexa, though she was reminding herself.

"Oh, look at that," Alexa commented, noticing her sister and Emily doing the downward dog. "Speaking of healthy habits, I need to get into some routine. I've fallen off lately."

"Don't worry dear, you'll get back to it. We've all spent a lot of energy dealing with other important matters lately, and we can't do it all."

"I know, Mum. Why are we so hard on ourselves?" Alexa asked, placing a hand on Jennie's shoulder.

"Perfectionists to the core," Jennie said. "We set ourselves up for failure."

"Right, because we all know there's no such thing as perfect," Alexa agreed. "Except when it comes to our Open House," she joked.

Chapter Ten

At almost four, Jennie moved a bowl of punch from the kitchen to the verandah, where it would stay cool. The cranberry punch sparkled in the cut glass, the deep red hue catching the light. Mindful of her back, Jennie lifted the bowl carefully and maneuvered it through the kitchen, living room, and hallway. She would grab the cups on her next trip, but for now, the punch was ready to make its grand entrance.

Thinking ahead, Jennie had already opened the heavy outer door, and now used her hip to nudge the screen door aside. Just as she stepped onto the porch, Rollo came barreling past her like a furry torpedo, as he launched into chasing a grey squirrel. Startled, Jennie barely had time to react before the punch bowl slipped from her grasp, crashing to the floor with a heart-stopping thud. The Christmas punch spilled in a dramatic arc, pooling among the jagged pieces of glass and scattered fruit garnishes. Vibrant red liquid splattered her legs, turning her into a canvas of festive chaos. Jennie gasped, her heart racing as she glanced around, hoping no one else had seen the calamity.

But the cheerful atmosphere shifted as the sound of shattering glass and Jennie's startled gasp echoed outside the house, drawing family members toward the verandah. Flustered, Jennie crouched down, trying to gather her thoughts and salvage the situation.

"Oh no, this is a disaster," she muttered, her cheeks flushing as she grabbed a nearby cloth and soaked up the mess.

Nick hurried to the verandah, a grin spreading across his face at the sight of the punch bowl disaster. "Looks like I'm not the only one who needs a drink, Mom!" he joked, gesturing at the chaos.

Emily appeared next, her eyes wide with both concern and amusement. "What happened?" she asked, hurrying over to help.

"Nothing we can't fix," Jennie replied. "If this is the worst that can happen, we're in for an amazing event."

Together, they began cleaning up the crimson disaster, their laughter blending with the distant strains of the band warming up, setting the stage for an unforgettable evening.

...

The clatter of Stewart Owen's pony cart rolling up the driveway thrilled Emily and the rest of the clean-up crew. Dressed in full Santa attire, Stewart had turned his cart into a festive spectacle, with amber lights outlining the seats and candy canes crisscrossing the back.

"This is incredible!" Emily exclaimed, standing up to get a better view. Her heart raced with utter joy at the sight.

"Stewart's pony cart has been a cherished part of the Mitchell family's Open House for as long as I can remember,"

Jennie said, beaming with pride. "It feels like a living link to the past."

As Joker, the pony, trotted up the driveway wearing a soft cedar wreath with a bright red bow around his neck, Emily felt a surge of delight. She realized this was more than just a ride—it was a Christmas tradition lovingly upheld for years. Beaming, she turned to Nick and Jennie, unable to contain her enthusiasm. "Who gets the first ride?"

Nick grinned and shot back, saying, "Definitely Grandma."

"And you're right, Nick," Jennie chimed. "It wouldn't be the same without Mom taking the first ride."

"It's so special that you keep these cherished customs alive," Emily said.

Just then, Kathleen stepped out in her coziest winter coat and matching hat, her eyes glowing with pure delight. Emily could see the joy radiating from her grandmother as Santa Stewart waved toward the verandah.

"Ho ho ho!" he called out, pulling his black-and-white Welsh pony to a halt before them.

Emily smiled as Nick linked his arm with Kathleen's, guiding her down the steps. He helped as she climbed into the pony cart and settled beside Stewart. The band struck up "Jingle Bells," filling the air with the festive tune as the pony cart circled the outdoor Christmas tree, then headed toward the corral, where they would have plenty of room for a delightful ride.

At that moment, surrounded by family and tradition, Emily knew deep down that this was what the holiday season should be about—sharing joy, creating happy memories, and honouring the past. It was a stark contrast to her experiences back home in England. While she still cared deeply for those she had left behind, the laughter and warmth here filled her with a sense of belonging she hadn't felt in a long time.

A troupe of community volunteers arrived, friendly and eager to help. Their job was to keep the tables stocked with food, drink, and anything else needed. A donation box by the verandah steps, with all proceeds this year to help buy new playground equipment for Chickadee Elementary School.

Jennie allowed herself a last stroll around the grounds to ensure everything was ready... at least, that is what she told everyone. But her true purpose was to experience the joy and gratitude that filled her every year during the holiday season. She walked alone, her favorite way to experience moments deeply and meaningfully, allowing her thoughts to unfold in the quiet.

The vibrant colours of the decorations and the faint sounds of laughter in the distance enveloped her like a warm embrace, grounding her in the festive atmosphere. The barn roof had already been lit up, though it wasn't dark yet. The bright pink lights, a fresh touch for this year, contrasted playfully with the weathered grey boards—it was impossible to resist turning them on early. Besides, the Christmas tree light-up would bring a new excitement when night fell.

Outside the wide barn doors, Jennie admired Clay's handiwork. He had hitched Music to an old wooden wagon from a shed near the site of the original homestead, and what he did next endeared him to her even more.

Clay outlined each spoked wheel with amber-coloured lights and looped wide red ribbons into clusters of bows, centering each arrangement on the wheel hubs. In the center of the wagon, he placed a small Christmas tree, its luminous red bulbs scattered evenly throughout the fir branches. Long strands of red and white ribbons gathered at the top, draped gracefully down the tree, shimmering with gold glitter.

As Jennie's eyes swept over Clay's creation, she felt a new appreciation for him. Large presents wrapped in red foil and tied with broad green ribbons nestled among smaller gifts in cream-colored wrap and white bows. A snowman and a reindeer, both painted white, added a touch of charm to the display, while three tall candy canes anchored to the ground flanked the front end of the wagon. At the back, another potted fir, untouched by decorations, showcased its natural beauty.

Jennie's mind flashed back to the many times Clay had called her a natural beauty. Smiling to herself, she couldn't help but wonder if that was what he had in mind when he placed the rogue tree beside the decorated wagon. He had given her that compliment repeatedly, and it lingered in her mind like a cherished gift.

Jennie paused at the horse corral where Music pranced, perhaps eager to greet Joker. Her decorated mane and tail held perfectly, and Jennie knew Alexa would wait to place his flower garland at just the right moment. The sparkling green saddle pad caught the light, adding a touch of magic to the festively adorned horse. Clay and Patrick set up floodlights in the dark spots so guests could admire all the decorations. But tonight, the moon shone brightly, and Jennie took it as a sign of good things ahead. Yet, beneath the joy, a faint flicker of worry still lingered around Nick and Emily. She wouldn't let it cloud the festivities, though.

"Boys," Jennie called out to the musicians, "please remember, at the end of your last set, play 'Have the Last Dance with Me.' You might remember the tradition from last year."

"We know, we know, Jennie," the banjo player piped up. "It's the last dance for the guests, but also, Stewart and Kathleen take the last pony ride of the evening, signaling the end of the show—uh, I mean, the event," he corrected with a laugh. "I've been down this road before."

"Perfect. Thank you so much. Just give me a heads-up so I can help Mom get ready," Jennie said, studying the playlist.

"And will you and Clay dance the first dance?" the piano player asked, a playful grin spreading across his face.

"Only if you start with 'Rockin' Around the Christmas Tree," same as always," Jennie replied, playing along.

"That always gets the party started," the piano player chuckled.

Continuing her stroll, Jennie admired the old-fashioned sleigh next to the tall fir tree that would be illuminated as it turned dark. She'd been too busy to have a good look, bustling about the verandah and kitchen, and now her eyes smiled with delight as she enjoyed the intricacies of the sleigh decorations. Snow-frosted evergreen gathered and tied with giant silver jingle bells graced the front section of the sleigh. Resting on the tufted red leather upholstery was an inviting red plaid blanket. A long, narrow pillow, off-white with large red letters reading "HOHOHO", rested against the seat back, adding a touch of humour to the scene. And under the giant fir tree, gingerbread men, teddy bears, and toy trains added to the fun.

Walking down the long driveway, Jennie looked toward the farm gate. Closer now, she admired a vintage wooden wagon inside the entrance. Thick evergreen garlands draped across the wooden box, tied with red velvet bows. The original welcome sign made by Jennie's grandfather, John, stood propped up for guests to see as they arrived. Jennie reflected on her heritage and the 'do-it-yourself' traditions passed down through the generations.

As she returned up the driveway, Jennie glanced at an old wooden wagon wheel painted red, propped against the chicken coop. Beside it, a small cedar tree rested on the weathered table they had unearthed from a crumbling shed long ago. Its multi-coloured lights cast a merry warmth over the otherwise dull area of the farm. A red lantern hanging from a nearby branch added to the rustic charm. The coop's narrow door held a wreath wrapped in candy-cane ribbon, two shiny red bells glinting at its center.

Moving toward the verandah, Jennie smiled with pleasure. The pink lights on the barn roof matched the ones wound around the verandah rails. *What would Dad think of this?* she mused, recalling her father's knack for innovation.

Cheerful pots of pink and white poinsettias framed the entrance to the house from the verandah. Sprigs of holly, bright red berries encased behind glass, adorned the hurricane lamps on the food tables.

"I think we're ready," Jennie announced, more to herself than anyone listening. Alexa and Kyla stepped onto the verandah, ready to greet their guests. Nick stood at the bottom of the driveway, directing the first arrivals to park in the field, ensuring the decorated grounds remained clear. Once the initial vehicles lined up, he knew the rest would follow suit. Jennie smiled, delighted to watch Kyla and Alexa interact with the newcomers. "We are so glad you could join us!" Alexa exclaimed, shaking hands with the owner of the Treehouse Café.

"Marianne," Kyla said to a dear friend. "It's been far too long!"

Jennie caught the spark of excitement in Kyla's eyes as her new boyfriend and former employer, Dr. Harry Nicholls, made his way up the verandah steps. His confident stride and friendly smile radiated warmth, instantly drawing attention. Although Jennie had met him once before during Rollo's raccoon incident, this was Harry's first visit to Cliffhouse, and she could sense it meant a lot to Kyla. As they embraced, Jennie prepared to welcome Harry to the celebration.

"Harry, so nice to see you again," Jennie said warmly. "Please make yourself at home."

"I've heard so much about this place and your famous

Open House," Harry replied, his gaze sweeping over the beautifully decorated grounds. "Thank you so much for having me, and nice to see you again, Jennie."

After excusing herself and weaving through the crowd, Jennie overheard a guest whispering to another.

"Is that...?" The woman pointed toward Harry, prompting Jennie to follow her gaze. "Dr. Nicholls? I didn't know he was dating Kyla."

"Surprise!" the other guest replied, her eyes sparkling with mischief. "They've been keeping it under wraps, but tonight it's as obvious as Kyla's baby bump," she remarked.

Jennie bristled at the implications of their schoolgirl-like comments, but she refused to let their snide remarks dampen the festive mood. When Dr. Kevin Hunter, Alexa's boyfriend, arrived, Jennie returned to the verandah to greet him.

"Mom," Alexa said, beaming, "I'd like you to meet Kevin, my date for the evening." Jennie noticed Alexa hesitated to introduce Kevin as her boyfriend. *Too early in the game, maybe,* Jennie mused.

"We're so glad you could join us, Kevin. Please make yourself at home."

Jennie turned toward the driveway as Stewart called out to Joker, "Giddy up!" Nick and Emily had volunteered to help guests settle into the pony cart, which was a big hit, especially with the kids.

Bev arrived next, her bright red hair shimmering in the verandah lights. A necklace of Christmas lights twinkled around her neck, amplifying her burst of festive energy. "Let's get this party started!" she called to Jennie, signalling it was time for her and Clay to take to the floor for the first dance.

Under the moonlit sky, Jennie and Clay stepped onto the dance floor, ready to kick off the celebrations. The guests hushed, their eyes turning to the couple as Clay nodded to the musicians, and the first notes of "Rockin' Around the Christmas Tree" filled the air.

"Are you ready?" Clay asked with a twinkle in his eye.

"Always," Jennie replied, her heart racing with excitement as they jived to the lively tune, their enthusiasm infectious.

Just then, Alexa stepped in with Music, the crowd gasping in admiration. The horse looked majestic, a soft evergreen spray cascading down her side. Interspersed among the greenery were vibrant red and champagne-coloured flowers, accented by bows of red and gold, making Music appear like a living decoration—a stunning blend of beauty and grace.

Soon, people shed their hats, wool scarves, and even some coats, enjoying the newfound freedom of movement. After the first set, Jennie turned to Clay.

"Let's take a break, honey, and make room for others, shall we?" Her two-piece pantsuit shimmered with sequins as she moved.

"Good idea, dear. I think it's time to light the Christmas tree. The full moon is bright and this is about as dark as it gets."

They walked over to the truck where the band was playing, requesting to borrow the microphone before the next tune. Jennie's excitement grew as she watched Clay head toward the verandah. He was adding bottles of sparkling wine to a table already adorned with as many champagne glasses as the rental company could provide. When she saw Clay's wave signaling that everything was ready, Jennie waited for the song to finish before stepping up to the microphone.

Ladies and gentlemen," she began, "there's a glass of bubbly—or sparkling water if you prefer—waiting for you on the verandah." We have drinks for the kids too, and they might want to bring a special treat. Now, please gather around the Christmas tree for the light-up when you are ready." With that, she made her way toward the verandah to join the others.

The band resumed playing Christmas music as laughter and excited chatter floated from the verandah, where tables displayed an enticing spread of finger foods. Platters of bacon-wrapped dates, creamy crab-artichoke dip, sweet potato bites, and flaky spinach puffs filled the air with savory aromas, drawing in guests nearby. Yet, Kathleen's famous sausage roll wreath elicited the most oohs and ahs. Jennie chuckled as Patrick's eyes widened with delight, declaring it "heaven on a plate."

The crowd gathered around the towering fir tree, anticipating the lighting ceremony. "How will Patrick know when to flick the lights?" Jennie asked Clay, suddenly recalling that important detail.

"Kathleen will turn them on when Patrick tells her to," he replied with a grin.

Jennie beamed at the thought of her mother doing the honours and returned to the band, taking her place at the microphone once more. She waited for the crowd to quiet before raising her glass in a toast. "To family and friends," she called out, her voice filled with emotion. "And to our beloved community of Sunrise Island."

As the crowd raised their glasses, the Christmas tree lit up in a glorious array of multicolored lights. Cheers and laughter erupted from the crowd as some hugged each other, while young children jumped up and down with joy.

Jennie and Clay danced through another set, and Jennie realized how much more relaxed she felt, knowing there was enough food and drink, and that people were enjoying themselves as she had hoped. Yet, she noticed Emily lingering at the edge of the crowd, her expression clouded with a look that tugged at Jennie's heart.

"Clay," she whispered, "I'd like to introduce Emily to some of our friends if you don't mind."

"Ah, mother hen is at it again," Clay chuckled. "But yes, I think some strategic introductions could help her with her struggles," he added, his words slightly slurred.

Jennie raised her brows. "Maybe ease up on the whiskey a bit, dear?" she suggested. "So, we can dance the last dance together, right?"

As they walked hand in hand across the grounds, Jennie spotted Bev engaged in animated conversation with a well-known local landscape artist. *I'll have a hard time pulling Bev away from him,* Jennie thought to herself.

Scanning the crowd for Emily, Jennie found her in the kitchen, about to carry a plate of hors d'oeuvres to the verandah. "Emily, how sweet of you to help! But I hope you have been enjoying the festivities too," she said.

"I have," Emily replied. "It's a joy to see your family's beautiful traditions firsthand. I'll remember them forever," she added.

"It's our pleasure, Emily. And, by the way, if you have a minute, I'd like to run something by you," Jennie said, beckoning her toward the home office for some privacy.

"What is it, Jennie?" Emily asked as they settled into their chairs.

"You know," Jennie began, "I've been thinking about what you told us about your father, and if it's okay with you, I'd like to introduce you to a few of my friends who have gone through similar struggles. They might be able to help you." Jennie smiled warmly as she waited for Emily's reply.

"Oh, uh, well, I'm just not sure that I want people to think of me as the woman with the father who's a substance misuser, you know?"

"I understand, Emily. It's only natural that you'd have that concern. "But believe me, I have many friends—more than just one—who are dealing with similar struggles or have faced similar situations in the past."

"Really? On this island?" Emily asked, her eyes wide.

"Yes," Jennie replied. "Starting with my best friend Bev. She was married to an alcoholic for ten years before she had enough."

"Bev? That bubbly, take-charge woman I met at the market?" Emily asked.

"The same," Jennie replied. "If I can drag her away from Mr. Handsome and Famous, we can chat. Nothing major—just a start. Is that okay, Emily?"

With Emily's agreement, Jennie left Emily behind, hoping to ask for Bev's help.

"Oh, Bev!" she beckoned. "Could you come and help me with something for a minute?" she called, hoping to drag her away from the handsome landscape painter.

Jennie smiled as Bev approached and got right to the point. "You met Nick's girlfriend at the Christmas market, Bev. Do you remember?"

I sure do, Jen. Nick's like a son to me, so of course I'm keeping a close eye on who he's dating," she said with a half-smile.

"Well," Jennie explained, "I think you two might have something in common."

"You remember my dear friend Bev, Emily? I think you two might have a lot to share."

Jennie's heart warmed as Bev smiled, her eyes kind. "It's great to see you again, Emily. I, too, have faced some tough times, so I'm here if you ever want to talk."

Jennie felt relieved as Emily chatted with Bev, the two women falling into easy conversation. They planned to meet after Christmas to share their stories.

Jennie didn't stop there. "Hey, Emily, come meet some of

my friends," she said, introducing guests whose experiences might provide a comforting perspective. She introduced Emily to the Wilsons, whose son had died from his heroin addiction, and to Carrie Munroe, whose father had been an addict for seventeen years. Dr. Shelley was there, too, so Jennie introduced the two, knowing Dr. Shelley had firsthand experience with addiction in her family, too.

"Now," Jennie said, squeezing Emily, "would you and Nick care to join Clay and me for the second-to-last pony ride of the night?"

...

"This place is even more stunning than I imagined," Jennie heard someone say as the evening wound down. She rose on her tiptoes and kissed Clay gently on the lips.

"Now," Jennie said, as the band began *Save the Last Dance for Me,* "let's waltz into the moonlight and say goodnight to our friends."

"Nick and Emily should be here," Clay said, glancing around.

"Maybe they're having their last dance in private," Jennie replied, looking to her right. There, she saw Nick and Emily helping Kathleen settle beside Stewart for their own "last dance" of the night.

"Aw, look, Clay! I'm surprised Mom could stay awake this late, but she wouldn't have wanted to miss this special moment. Besides, she wisely napped for a couple of hours so she would enjoy the ride."

The warmth of the evening wrapped around Jennie and Clay as they shared the last dance. With her heart full of joy and hope, Jennie felt that this year's Open House would blend tradition and new beginnings.

Chapter Eleven

The rooster's crow at sunrise failed to wake anyone on Christmas Eve, but that didn't mean there wasn't still much to do before the big day. Jennie was the first up, taking in the aftermath of another successful Open House.

"Where are the volunteers when we need them most?" she joked to Clay as he appeared with a steaming cup of coffee and began adjusting the heat lamps on the verandah.

"This is what success looks like, huh, Jen?" he said with a laugh.

"How about you, Patrick, and Nick handle the clean-up while the rest of us help Mom prepare for our Christmas Eve dinner tonight?"

"You always were the organized one," Clay said, pulling her in for a quick squeeze.

...

Emily stretched from head to toe before getting out of bed.

Just as she was about to rise, Nick pulled her back, wanting her to snuggle for a moment longer.

"Ah, sorry, Nick, but we have a lot to do today, and honestly, I'm a little tired—in a good way—after the Open House, but I need to get moving," she said, giving him a quick kiss on his lips.

Emily headed to the bathroom, turning on the shower, anticipating the usual morning buzz in the farmhouse kitchen.

When she finished showering, she noticed Nick had left the room. A pang of sadness washed over her as she gazed at the empty bed, its covers in disarray—like the aftermath of an earthquake, with everything shifted, perhaps changing lives forever.

...

The comforting aromas of Christmas dinner filled the kitchen. In the Mitchell family tradition, they enjoyed their turkey on Christmas Eve, allowing them to relax on Christmas Day after the main cooking was done.

"Your own savory, no doubt," Emily teased Kathleen as she sniffed a fresh sprig on the kitchen island.

Kathleen smiled with pride. "The secret ingredient in the stuffing," she said. "It's hard to come by, so we grow our own."

"Well, I'm excited to try your famous stuffing," Emily said. "And if you still want to try my sticky toffee pudding, I'd better get cracking."

"And I can't wait to try your dessert, Emily. A taste of England is just what we need here at Cliffhouse," she teased.

...

Nick closed the greenhouse door behind him, his bare

hands chilled from the evening air. Holding a long-stemmed white rose, he paused, glancing toward the warm light from the kitchen window. Inside, Emily moved effortlessly, her laughter mingling with the voices of his family. It felt natural, as though she was already woven into the rhythm of Cliffhouse life. A sense of contentment settled over him—this was where he wanted to be and where he wished Emily would find her place.

As Nick headed into the house, he handed the rose to Emily. "For you, my lady love," he said, kissing her.

"Such a beautiful rose, Nick—thank you," Emily said, looking around for a vase.

"Here's a bud vase from last night," Kathleen said, handing it to Emily.

After waiting for her to fill the crystal vase with water and add some eucalyptus for greenery, Nick took Emily's hand as they climbed the stairs to get dressed for the evening.

Nick carefully laid out his white shirt and black tie on the bed, glancing sideways at Emily as she draped her red velvet dress over the closet door. He admired the elegant curve of her shoulders and how her black lacey undergarments contrasted her porcelain skin.

Instinctively, he moved to her, slipping his arms around her waist from behind. He brushed a kiss against her neck, inhaling the familiar scent of her perfume. He felt Emily relax against him, her body molding into his as if they were two parts of the same whole.

"I can't wait for us to spend Christmas together next year," he murmured, his voice low. "And the year after. I love our life here."

Nick felt a surge of warmth, the future he imagined for them stretching out in front of him, clear and bright. But when Emily turned her face slightly, her eyes closed, he felt a flicker of hesitation from her—a shadow he couldn't quite name. Still, she stayed in his arms, and that was all the reassurance he needed.

What Nick couldn't see—couldn't feel—was the turmoil simmering beneath Emily's calm exterior. He wasn't privy to the secret she carried, the one gnawing at her from inside. He didn't know that she hadn't told him the whole truth and that she faced her family's darkness alone.

Chapter Twelve

The comforting aroma of roast turkey filled the farmhouse, mingling with the earthy scent of cedar boughs decorating the dining area. Breakfast was simple this morning; all the focus was on the late afternoon feast that would carry them well into the evening."

Kathleen reigned as the undisputed queen of the kitchen. She moved gracefully between the counters, stirring pots, checking on the turkey, and keeping a close eye on her famous stuffing. Emily had been hearing about it for weeks—the stuffing that even the pickiest eaters go back for seconds. But people were fiercely loyal to their family's stuffing recipes, Emily thought. For her, that meant a dense, chestnut-flavoured stuffing that the English enjoyed spreading on toast the next morning.

"Emily, come over here and have a taste," Kathleen said, beckoning her over with a wave of her wooden spoon.

Emily stepped forward, curious to see what all the fuss was about. She took a small bite, the flavours bursting in her mouth

—a blend of savory and sweet, with a hint of rosemary and something she couldn't quite place.

"This is incredible," Emily said, her eyes widening in surprise.

Kathleen's face lit up with pride. "It's an old family recipe," she explained. "My grandmother made it every Christmas, and we've kept it going ever since."

Emily nodded, feeling both honoured and slightly envious. She had always longed for traditions like these to tie her to a place and a family. Her memories of Christmas were far less comforting—holidays spent pretending everything was fine while chaos simmered beneath the surface. Here, the Mitchells embraced their traditions with open hearts and full bellies. She wished she could be part of it, wished for more time beyond June, but reality tugged at her, pulling her back like a cruel force.

Alexa and Kyla moved in and out of the kitchen, setting dishes on the long wooden dining table.

Jennie made it clear— Patrick and Emily were off kitchen duty—and Nick took it to mean he was, too.

Emily stood beside Patrick, listening as Nick pointed out Christmas tree decorations. The afternoon sun cast a warm glow, catching the glitter of a team of reindeer pulling Santa's sleigh. Each ornament seemed to have a story, and now and then, Jennie and Kathleen would pop in to share its significance —a vacation in the mountains, a relative who had passed away, a cherished memory. Emily felt spellbound, listening and watching, as if she were on the verge of something wonderful yet not quite a part of it. Moving to the largest window, Emily gazed at the frost-covered pastures of the Mitchell family farm. It was her first Christmas Eve here, and she had tried to brace herself for the whirlwind of traditions, laughter, and stories.

But nothing could have prepared her for the warmth that seemed to infuse every corner of this house.

"A white Christmas just for you, Em," Nick said, joining her at the window. "It doesn't snow here very often, especially at Christmastime, just when you'd want it," he said, chuckling.

"It's beautiful," Emily murmured, admiring the big, fluffy snowflakes dusting the evergreens across the property. "Like something out of a storybook," she said, glancing toward the kitchen as Clay entered the dining room.

Emily grabbed her phone, hoping to capture a photo of Clay, all smiles, as he balanced a golden-brown turkey on a massive platter—a family heirloom.

"Make way for the bird!" he called out, his deep voice carrying over the clatter of pots and pans.

"Let's be seated, everyone!" Kathleen chimed in as they all made their way to the festive table, some cheering at the feast before them. Emily couldn't help but smile at the vibrant energy filling the room.

It was a lively affair, with stories and laughter flowing as freely as the wine. Kathleen's stuffing lived up to its reputation, while the turkey was tender and flavourful. Emily was swept up in the warmth and joy around her, almost able to forget her worries.

After the main course, she rallied Nick and Patrick to clear the dishes. "That'll give me time to set out the carrot pudding and sauces," Kathleen declared.

"Carrot pudding?" Emily asked Nick, who had come up beside her.

"It's a big deal around here," he replied with a grin. "My great-grandmother passed down the recipe. It's not Christmas without it."

Emily smiled, but her heart sank a little. It wasn't just about the pudding or the stuffing—it was about the stories, the traditions, and the threads that held this family together. She wondered if Nick could sense the sadness she couldn't quite hide, even as she tried to savour each moment.

The others had shifted their chairs away from the table, taking a breather after the heavy dinner. A few headed out onto the veranda, while others ventured into the snow, hoping there was enough to build a snowman.

Once the dishwasher was loaded and running, Jennie was asked to ring the dinner bell on the veranda. As she did, Kathleen entered the dining area, carrying a steaming mound of carrot pudding, with Jennie behind her, balancing the sauces.

"Nick, will you do the honors this year?" Jennie asked when everyone had gathered back around the dining table.

Emily could hardly wait to see what the family had in store. She watched with curiosity as Nick retrieved a bottle of brandy from the liquor cabinet and poured the amber liquid over the steaming mound of pudding.

"Dim the lights, please, Em?" Nick asked. As she turned the switch, golden and blue flames flickered to life around the Christmas pudding, lit by Nick with a long-handled lighter. Emily smiled with delight as oohs, ahs, and knowing smiles rose from the table—a tradition as cherished as the pudding itself.

"Now, for those of you not familiar with carrot pudding," Kathleen called out, glancing toward Emily and Patrick, "there are two sauces to choose from—lemon, for a tangy sweetness, and hard sauce, for a rich, buttery brandy flavor. Let me know which one you like best."

"Richness upon richness," Nick teased. "Are you ready for the intensity of this tiny mound, Em?"

Emily drizzled lemon sauce over her serving of warm carrot pudding, then placed a small scoop of sugary hard sauce beside it. As she brought the spoon to her mouth, the room fell silent, and all eyes were on her; she felt like a famous chef on a TV show tasting their creation.

"This has nothing to do with carrots," she declared, drawing laughter from the others. She turned to Patrick.

"Have you ever tasted anything so delectable?"

"Not in my entire life," he replied, grinning. "Kathleen, you've outdone yourself—if that's possible."

"Plum pudding, move over," Emily said, savouring the spicy sweetness of the moist dessert. She didn't dare ask for the recipe.

After dinner, when they gathered in the living room for the Christmas Eve tradition of opening one gift, Emily's thoughts turned heavy again. She didn't belong here—not really. And soon enough, she would have to leave it all behind.

Trying to lift herself from the growing sadness, Emily searched for a gift to give Nick while the others picked their own. A bright green foil-wrapped present caught her eye, and, grateful for the distraction, she handed it to him, smiling warmly.

Emily glanced up, searching his eyes for a clue to what he had in mind. There was a quiet intensity there, making her heart race with uncertainty. So many questions swirled in her mind. Was this the moment Nick would reveal that he knew about her father, the real reason she was leaving? Would he try to stop her? Would he understand? For a fleeting moment, doubt crept in—had Jennie betrayed her trust? But she knew in her heart that Jennie would keep her word.

Chapter Thirteen

Nick stood beside Emily on the beach, the sunset casting warm hues over the water and wrapping the island in a soft glow. He glanced at her as the wind caught strands of her hair while she fixed her gaze on the horizon. She looked peaceful, yet there was a distant quality to her expression—something he couldn't quite grasp. He hoped that tonight would change that.

"This place..." Nick said softly, his voice carrying over the sound of the waves, "holds a special place in my heart, Em, just like you do."

Emily's lips curved into a small smile, but it felt fleeting. "It's beautiful," she replied, her voice quieter than usual.

Nick reached into his pocket, feeling the velvet ring box nestled there, his heart racing with anticipation. He had been planning this moment for weeks, envisioning the perfect time to ask the woman he loved to marry him. He knew she was worried about the future, but he hoped to show her they could face anything together. With her by his side, he believed there was nothing they couldn't overcome.

Taking a deep breath, Nick turned to Emily, his hands trembling slightly as he pulled out the box. "Emily, there's something I've been wanting to ask you for a long time."

Her eyes widened, and she remained silent, watching him steadily.

Nick dropped to one knee, the ring catching the last of the setting sun's light. "You make my life better every day. I can't imagine sharing it with anyone else, Emily... will you marry me?"

For a moment, everything seemed to hang in the air, suspended between the crash of the waves and the gentle whisper of the wind. Nick waited, his heart pounding, anticipating the joy, the laughter, the 'yes' he hoped would follow.

But Emily's expression changed. She took a step back, shaking her head. "Nick, I... I can't."

The words hit him like a rogue wave, stealing the breath from his lungs. He blinked, bewildered. "What? You... you can't?" He straightened, the ring still in his hand, feeling cold and useless now. "Why not?"

Emily's eyes brimmed with tears as she turned away, wrapping her arms around her body as if trying to hold it together.

"I love you, Nick, but I'm leaving. I'm going back to England as soon as we graduate in June."

Nick's heart sank. "England?" He stepped closer to her, trying to make sense of it all. "You're leaving me for a job offer, Emily?" He paused, kicking a piece of driftwood out to sea. "Look," he continued, his voice firm but strained, "we can set up our practice together here on Sunrise, just like we talked about. We can work toward having a diversified clinic if that's what you want."

Nick stared at Emily, stunned. This wasn't what they'd discussed last spring. She had told him she was considering staying, but she had to work out a few details first. Why was she springing this on him now?

"We never talked about this, Em," Nick said, his voice breaking. "I thought we were figuring things out here. You can't just decide something like this without me."

"I didn't want to hurt you." Emily's voice wavered, her hands shaking as she wiped at her eyes. "But this is something I need to do. I don't expect you to understand. And," she added, "I think you believed what you wanted to believe. I tried to tell you, but you didn't want to hear it."

Nick felt the weight of her words pressing down on him, suffocating the hope he'd carried with him to this moment. "So, you're leaving. You're just... going?"

Emily nodded, her expression heavy with guilt and regret. Tears streamed down her cheeks as she spoke.

"We have each other for six more months, but then I must say goodbye."

Nick's mind reeled. How could everything change so fast? He thought tonight marked the beginning of their future, and now she was telling him she'd already decided—without him.

"But Emily..." His voice broke as he reached out, taking her hand. "We can make this work. We can find a way for you to stay here and start our lives together."

"I'm sorry," she whispered, her voice trembling. "I wish things could be different."

Nick's chest tightened, frustration and disbelief boiling inside him like a storm ready to break.

"After everything we built together," he said, "the plans we made, you're just walking away?"

Her tears fell harder now, gripping Nick with sadness. Emily wrapped her arms around him, sobbing, but he didn't return the hug, his heart still searching for answers.

"It isn't about the job. It's about me doing the right thing—I have responsibilities at home that I simply cannot ignore."

"Em, I thought you were committed to us. What responsibilities? To your friends? Your family?

Emily looked away, her expression pained. "It's not just about them, Nick. It's about my dad. He's been struggling, and I must be there for my mum. I'm their only child... it's different from your family."

She took a shaky breath, her voice breaking. "I thought I could make it work here, but I can't just walk away from them. I love you, but I must take care of my family."

Nick felt the ground slipping from under him. The life he'd imagined with her—the home, the future, the family—they were disappearing before his eyes. He released himself from Emily's hold and stepped back, shaking his head.

"You won't even try to stay," he said, his voice barely above a whisper. "You've already made up your mind."

Emily bit her lip, unable to meet his gaze. "I'm so sorry. Nick, I love you, but I... I can't stay."

Nick closed the ring box slowly, his great-grandmother's ring now stripped of the love it once promised. He looked at Emily, searching for anything that might make sense, but all he saw was the widening distance between them.

He nodded, his throat tight. "I don't understand, Emily. But if this is what you've decided..." His voice cracked, and he had to swallow hard before finishing. "Then there's nothing more I can do."

Emily reached out, as if to touch him, but stopped short. "I wish things were different," she whispered.

Nick looked at her one last time, his heart breaking into pieces. He thought she was his future, but now she was walking away. Without another word, he turned and walked down the beach, leaving her standing there as the sun dipped below the horizon.

Chapter Fourteen

Jennie stood by the window, watching the snow flutter gently outside. From where she stood, she could hear the joyful chaos of her family preparing for dinner—the laughter, the clatter of dishes, the occasional teasing remark. But her gaze drifted to Nick, who stood on the verandah adjusting a string of lights. His movements were careful and mechanical as if concentrating on keeping his expression neutral.

Jennie turned back to the kitchen, where Emily was busy laying out the silverware on the table, her expression a mask of concentration. She seemed preoccupied, trying to dissolve into the task.

Nick stepped inside, brushing snow from his shoulders. He gave Jennie a tight smile, his gaze flicking briefly to Emily.

"The wind knocked a strand of lights loose last night," he said, his voice bright but with a strained edge.

"Thanks, love," Jennie managed, keeping her tone casual, but her heart ached beneath the surface. She wasn't sure what had happened, but something had shifted between them since last night. She had seen Nick head down to the beach with Emily in tow, and when they returned, he wore a guarded expression she hadn't seen in him for years. Emily looked pale as if whatever had passed between them had taken its toll. Even though Jennie found it painful to watch, she quickly shook off her concern, reminding herself that family gatherings were meant for joy, not worry.

"Just about time for tourtière," Jennie announced as everyone gathered around the dining table for another day of feasting and family fun.

After enjoying the savory pie, they took a short break, the air buzzing with anticipation for the much-loved sticky toffee pudding—done the English way. Jennie noticed Emily's effort to maintain a cheerful demeanor; despite the earlier tension, she smiled warmly as she introduced the dessert.

"This is a special treat in my family," Emily explained, her voice brightening. She shared that there were many variations of the original recipe, but this one had always been her parents' favourite.

"Oh, this is heavenly," Kathleen declared. "It's a prize-winner, Emily. Thank you so much for bringing this treat to our family celebration."

"Yes," Jennie agreed warmly. "I bet this will be a Cliffhouse tradition from now on." She paused, glancing at Emily, silently adding, *And I hope you'll be here to share it with us every year.*

The family then gathered in the living room for gift-giving, a ritual Jennie cherished. Clay passed around presents with dramatic flair, making everyone laugh with his over-the-top commentary.

Emily tried to focus on the moment, to be present with this family that had welcomed her so completely. When she opened her gift from Kathleen—a hand-knitted scarf in deep burgundy, the colour of winter berries—she felt tears sting her eyes. "Thank you," she whispered, her voice thick with emotion.

Emily stared at the present she knew was from Nick, her hands trembling slightly as she reached for it. Her pulse quickened, and she had to remind herself to breathe. Glancing up, she found Nick watching her. His eyes were soft, with a tender, familiar warmth.

Nick leaned in closer, keeping his voice low so only Emily could hear. "I love you, Em," he murmured. "Whatever happens, I just want you to know that.

Emily blinked back tears, unsure of what to say. She opened the box, her heart racing, and saw a delicate silver bracelet with a single, tiny charm—a seashell, one she recognized from the beach they often visited together. It was simple, beautiful, and full of meaning. It encapsulated everything they had shared, everything she was leaving behind.

"Nick," she began, her voice breaking, but he shook his head gently.

"It's okay," he said, though she could hear the pain in his voice. "Just... hold on to it, okay?"

Emily nodded, slipping the bracelet onto her wrist, and feeling its cool weight. Her eyes settled on the angel at the top of the Christmas tree, as if grounding herself in its steady presence. She wanted to hold on to this moment, to this family, to Nick—but deep down, she knew she couldn't.

They sat together in silence, surrounded by the rustle of wrapping paper and cheerful chatter. Yet, they felt isolated in their thoughts, last night's heartbreak still fresh. Emily felt the familiar ache in her chest, the sadness she had tried so hard to bury. This was supposed to be a time of joy and celebration, but all she could feel was the impending loss of everything she loved. Beside her, Nick still held onto a hope she could never give him.

As the hours passed, Jennie noticed the subtle signs in their behaviour—the way Nick's shoulders tensed every time Emily spoke, the way Emily kept her gaze averted when passing him a plate or a cup, and the silence stretching between them like an invisible barrier.

Jennie's instinct to intervene was almost overwhelming, but she held back. Whatever happened, they needed to work through it their way. Still, her heart ached to see her son's forced smiles, watching Emily's distant eyes and feeling the heaviness that hung in the air between them. *Has she not told him yet?*

...

Nick stood in the kitchen, running a dish towel over his hands, trying to steady himself. He could hear the murmur of voices from the living room. From where he stood, he had a clear view of Emily, sitting on the edge of the armchair, laughing with everyone else.

She played her part flawlessly, but Nick couldn't shake the feeling that they were both trapped in a scene with no exit. Last night's rejection still echoed in his mind, as sharp and cold as the winter wind. He replayed her words—*I think you believed what you wanted to believe*—each repetition cutting deeper than the last. "Nick, can you bring in the cider?" Jennie called, snapping him back to the present.

"Yeah, sure," he said, sounding normal like his world hadn't just crumbled. He poured the steaming cider into a ceramic pitcher, forcing his hands to stay steady, and carried it into the living room.

As he set the pitcher down, Emily glanced up, her eyes meeting his for a split second before she looked away. It was that brief flicker of guilt, or was it regret, that told him she was struggling, too. But it did nothing to ease the ache in his chest.

Throughout the day, he forced himself to laugh when Clay made jokes, nodded with Patrick about his plans, and smiled when his sisters showed off their new gifts. But every time he caught sight of Emily, his resolve weakened. He kept imagining what today could have been—a celebration of Christmas and their future together. He had pictured this day with a ring on her finger, sharing knowing smiles and planning for a life they both wanted.

Instead, there was only this distance between them, a silence that felt too heavy to lift. He caught Jennie watching him, her eyes full of questions she didn't ask. Nick tried to reassure her with a smile, but it felt like a lie. Everything felt like a lie today.

Emily excused herself to take a call in the hallway, and Nick watched her slip away, the heaviness of their unspoken truth settling between them. He had tried to give her space, hoping she would come to him and share what was troubling her. Her claim of responsibilities to her family over what he believed was their commitment to each other didn't add up. With each passing hour, his doubts deepened, gnawing at the hope he clung to. *What was she hiding?*

When Emily returned, her expression was composed, as if she'd steeled herself for whatever was coming next. Nick wanted to ask if she was alright, to close this gap between them, but he couldn't bring himself to say the words. He was afraid of what her answer might be, afraid that whatever was broken couldn't be fixed.

The rest of the day passed in a blur, a series of half-hearted conversations and strained laughter. As the evening ended and everyone gathered for the last toast, Nick felt like an outsider, watching the people he loved celebrate while he stood on the sidelines, wondering where it had all gone wrong.

Chapter Fifteen

Emily stood in front of the bathroom mirror, her hands gripping the sink as if it were the only thing keeping her upright. The dim light reflected the exhaustion in her eyes—nights of restless sleep and days of putting on a brave face. She had just gotten off another tense phone call with her mother, who was barely holding it together. Her father's addiction had reached a new low—unpaid bills were piling up, and they had received yet another eviction notice. Emily knew she couldn't stay on Sunrise Island and pretend everything was fine anymore.

Nick's proposal weighed heavily on her mind. She could still see the way his hopeful eyes dimmed when she hesitated and said she couldn't marry him. The words had felt like ashes in her mouth.

She splashed cold water on her face, the chill jolting her into the present moment. *I cannot do this alone anymore.* The realization rang in her mind like a relentless drumbeat.

...

Emily asked to borrow Kyla's Forester, needing time alone to process everything swirling inside her. As she drove into the village, she wandered, her feet guiding her toward the harbor. The peaceful atmosphere enveloped her like a comforting blanket, a welcome reprieve from her turbulent thoughts. Just as she was about to leave, Bev spotted her from across the street and waved with an enthusiasm that Emily couldn't ignore.

"Emily, there you are! I've been wanting to catch up," Bev said, her red hair catching the sunlight. Bev's bubbly personality and warm tone felt as inviting to Emily as the change of scene.

Bev tilted her head, taking in Emily's worn expression. "You don't look like yourself, love. What's going on?"

Emily tried to muster a convincing smile. "It's nothing, just... a lot on my mind."

"Doesn't sound like 'nothing' to me," Bev said. "Come on, let's grab a coffee."

It was a short stroll to the Treehouse Café, where they settled into a cozy corner table. Emily stirred her coffee absently, trying to find the words. Bev didn't press her, but her patient silence was a gentle nudge.

"It's my family," Emily finally admitted, her voice barely audible. "My dad... he's been missing for five days now, and my mum is beside herself. Bev, I'm all she has, and I don't know how to help them from here."

Bev's brow furrowed with concern as she processed Emily's words. She reached across the table, squeezing Emily's hand. "Oh, Emily. Are you carrying this all on your own?"

Emily nodded, feeling tears welling up. They soon turned into sobs she could no longer contain; she hadn't allowed herself to cry like this in so long.

"You know," Bev said gently, "you don't have to figure this

out yourself. There are people here who can help—people who know what it's like to deal with situations like this."

Emily shifted, still staring at the floor until Bev's words caused her to look up. "There are?"

"Of course, there are," Bev replied. "I know a couple of ladies in the community who've been through similar things. In fact," she added with a warm smile, "I'm one of them. We've got more wisdom from experience than you can imagine. Let's arrange a little get-together."

Chapter Sixteen

Nick placed his mug on the table, his fingers tracing the rim as he glanced at Emily. The farm kitchen was warm, with the scent of wood smoke and the soft murmur of music from the living room. Everyone else had gone to bed, leaving just the two of them in the lingering silence of the night.

Emily knew he sensed the distance between them and was waiting for her to speak. She turned her mug in her hands, feeling the steam warm her face as she gathered the courage she had been putting off for so long. There was no turning back; she couldn't carry this burden without him any longer.

"Nick," she began, her voice barely more than a whisper. She felt him look at her fully, his posture shifting, all his attention focused on her now. "There's something I haven't told you—something I was afraid to tell you."

Nick's eyebrows furrowed, and Emily could see the worry creeping into his expression. He reached for her hand across the table, his fingers gentle but firm. "You can tell me anything, Em. You know that, right?"

Emily swallowed hard, the words caught in her throat. She knew this would change how he saw her and their future—but she could not keep living in the shadow of her father's mistakes.

"It's about my dad," she said, her voice shaking despite her efforts to keep it steady. "He's...he's struggled with addiction for years. Heroin. It's been...awful, Nick. Addiction has trapped him for so long, and I—I couldn't tell you because I was afraid it would change everything."

Nick's hand tightened slightly around hers, but he didn't interrupt, letting her words fill the space between them.

"I was afraid that if you knew, you'd look at me differently," she continued, tears welling in her eyes. "I thought you'd see me as tainted or... or that it would hurt your reputation if we set up the practice together, and people found out about my family's mess."

Nick's expression softened, the tension melting away as he listened. He lifted her hand to his lips and gently kissed her knuckles, his touch anchoring her.

"Emily," he said, his voice steady and full of understanding. "You're not tainted. What others might think about your family's struggles doesn't matter to me. I love you for everything you've been through and for the beautiful soul you are."

Emily felt the dam inside her break, the relief mingling with guilt as a shaky breath escaped. "I should've told you sooner," she whispered, her voice thick with emotion. "But I was so scared of losing you."

Nick shook his head, his gaze unwavering. "I'm not going anywhere, Em. I know things are complex, but we're in this together. We'll find a way through, supporting your mum too."

Emily's tears spilled over, and Nick stood, pulling her into his arms. She felt the last of her defenses crumble as she leaned into him, letting the weight of her secret fall away.

For the first time in a long time, she felt like she wasn't carrying it all alone.

...

A few days later, Emily sat in Jennie's living room, where Bev had gathered a small group of women who knew about coping with family crises. There was Nancy, whose husband had battled alcoholism for years before finding recovery, and Maggie, who had grown up with an addicted father and learned how to protect her peace.

At first, Emily felt awkward and out of place, but as the women shared their stories, she felt her guard crumble. They spoke openly about their own experiences—the shame, the fear, and the helplessness that came with loving someone caught in the grip of addiction.

"I spent years thinking I had to fix everything," Nancy said, her voice steady. "But truthfully, you can't pour from an empty cup. You've got to care for yourself first, or you won't be any good to anyone else."

Emily listened, her heart aching at the familiar words. She had been so focused on holding her family together that she had forgotten to care for herself. And now, faced with the reality of leaving Sunrise Island and Nick behind, she felt completely lost.

"Emily," Maggie said softly, "you don't have to decide anything right now. But whatever you choose, make sure it's what's best for *you*, not just everyone else."

For the first time in a long time, Emily felt understood. She wasn't alone in this—others had walked this path before her, and they would help her find her way.

Chapter Seventeen

Back at Cliffhouse, Emily stared at her phone, the message from her mother still open, the words burning into her mind. *He's gone, Em. I can't do this on my own anymore. I reported him missing.*

The emptiness in her mother's words echoed in Emily's heart. Her father had been in and out of their lives for so long that she thought she was prepared for this—another disappearance, another crisis. But seeing it written out so plainly made it feel final in a way it hadn't before.

She sat at the kitchen table, staring at the snow-covered fields, seeking calm. But her chest felt tight, and the weight of everything she had carried over these past months seemed to close in on her. The farmhouse, normally alive with warmth and energy, felt impossibly silent and distant.

A knock on the back door jolted her from her thoughts. Emily wiped her eyes quickly and tried to compose herself. When she opened the door, Bev stood there, bundled in a thick winter coat, her cheeks flushed from the cold.

"Hey, Em," Bev said softly, her eyes full of concern. "Mind if I come in?"

Emily stepped aside, grateful for the company even though she didn't feel like chatting. Bev removed her coat and settled into one of the kitchen chairs. She was quiet, her gaze studying Emily's face as if searching for the right words.

"Nick mentioned you heard from your mum," Bev began as if testing the waters. "How are you holding up?"

Emily sighed, the knot in her chest loosening slightly at the mention of her mother. She hadn't told Nick much, but he knew her well enough to guess something was wrong. "Not great," she admitted. "He's gone again, and Mum... she's reported him missing."

Bev reached across the table, her fingers warm and firm around Emily's hand. "I'm so sorry, Em."

Emily nodded, feeling the tears building again. She took a deep breath, trying to keep her composure. "I just don't know what to do," she confessed. "I feel like I'm abandoning her by staying here."

Bev's eyes softened. "Listen, love. We all know how much you care about your mum, and you've been doing everything you can to support her. But she needs more than just phone calls and visits. Maybe it's time she had a real fresh start—a place that feels safe. Somewhere like here."

Emily looked up, confusion flickering in her eyes. "Here? On the island?"

Bev nodded. "Why not? Sunrise Island isn't just for vacationers and tourists; it's a community. It's a place for healing, too. Many folks here understand what it's like to shoulder someone else's struggles. We've all faced tough times and support each other through them."

The words, "someone else's struggles", struck a chord with

Emily. For so long, she had felt trapped under the weight of her parents' issues, convinced it was her burden to bear.

She paused, allowing Bev's words to sink in. As she eventually turned her thoughts to the idea of her mother moving to Sunrise, she shook her head, doubt creeping in. "I don't know if she'd leave England. It's where she's lived her whole life. And, as hopeless as it seems, she'd never give up on Dad."

"But what kind of life is that for her now?" Bev's voice was gentle but firm. "You said yourself that she's struggling, especially now with your dad reported missing. Maybe this change is what she needs. You're already here, Em, building a life and finding your footing. Perhaps it's time your mum joined you. And, who knows, maybe your father would join her, somewhere down the line. It's impossible to predict how that might unfold."

Emily felt something stir within her—a tiny spark of hope, a new possibility. She hadn't considered asking her mother to come to the island. It seemed too drastic, too much of an upheaval. But maybe that's what her mother needed. Perhaps Emily would find peace in helping her mother find a new path.

Bev gave her a reassuring smile. "Think about it, Emily. Talk to Nick, talk to Jennie. They'll help you figure it out. And if your mum's open to the idea, we'll all be here to welcome her."

* * *

The next few days were a blur of conversations and plans. Nick was supportive when Emily brought up the idea of Charlotte coming to the island and the thought of offering her a place to find peace thrilled Jennie. They discussed logistics, preparations, and how they could prepare for Lottie's visit should she decide to come. Emily knew that her mother would hesitate to leave the only home she had ever known.

But as they spoke, Emily felt something she hadn't in a long time—a glimmer of hope.

* * *

In the early morning, Emily and Nick sat on the verandah, sipping coffee as the sun rose over the snow-dusted fields. The morning's stillness reflected the calmness that enveloped Emily, a welcome change from the turmoil she had felt before.

"Do you think she'll come?" Emily asked, her voice barely above a whisper.

Nick reached over and took her hand, his fingers warm against the chill of the morning. "I think she will, Em," he said, smiling. "And if she doesn't, we'll figure it out. But at least she'll know she has options."

Emily nodded, clarity settling within her as she watched the light spread over the fields. For the first time, she felt a shift —realizing that *she*, too, had always had options, even if they'd been hard to see. They sat in comfortable silence, watching the sun rise higher, its light casting the promise of new beginnings.

Chapter Eighteen

I t was late January when Lottie arrived on the island. Emily stood at the ferry dock, her heart racing as the boat approached. Nick stood beside her, his hand steady on her back, offering silent support.

As Lottie stepped off the ferry, Emily noticed the exhaustion etched on her mother's face, a testament to the long flight and undoubtedly to her most recent struggles back home. Yet there was something more—a flicker of relief perhaps, or a glimmer of hope that this place might offer a fresh start. Their embrace was so tight that the distance of six months apart melted away; for the first time in what felt like ages, words weren't necessary.

"Welcome to Sunrise Island, Mum," Emily said, her voice thick with emotion, her heart swelling at the sight of her mother.

Lottie's lips curved into a small, hesitant smile, a spark of warmth illuminating her features.

"Thank you, love," she replied, her voice soft and filled

with unspoken feelings as if she were savouring the moment of reunion.

Emily felt proud as Nick extended his hand to her mother, their handshake marking a moment she had never dared to imagine. Seeing them together on Sunrise Island, especially under such happy and hopeful circumstances, filled her with wonder.

They drove to the farm, where Jennie and Kathleen had prepared a room for Lottie, and set out tea and homemade scones in the kitchen. The farmhouse, full of warmth and history, seemed to captivate Lottie as she stepped inside.

Over the following days, Emily introduced her mother to the island community—Bev, Jennie, and the others who had become Emily's lifeline. They welcomed Lottie with open arms, offering support and understanding without judgment. Lottie was hesitant at first, but slowly, she opened up, sharing pieces of her story in quiet conversations over tea and long walks along the beach.

And as Emily watched her mother find her footing, a renewed sense of purpose took hold. Emily had spent countless hours trying to help, wrestling with her sense of responsibility and hope. But now, on the cusp of a new beginning, she felt a steady resolve—to support her mother in reclaiming her life, free to focus on the present. It was time for Lottie to start living with strength and peace, and Emily was determined to be by her side, every step of the way.

Emily stood on the beach, stepping back when the waves came too close to her feet. The tide danced playfully at her ankles, a gentle reminder of the ocean's ebb and flow. Nick joined her, slipping his hand into hers, their fingers intertwining like the roots of the island's ancient trees. They stood in silence, watching the sunset paint the sky in shades of pink and gold, the horizon a canvas of their unspoken dreams.

"I think she's going to stay," Emily said, smiling, barely able to contain her joy.

Nick turned to her, his eyes full of tenderness for the love of his life. "And you?" he asked, joking.

Emily gazed at the ocean, the cool breeze brushing her face and the solid ground beneath her feet. For the first time in a long while, she felt a sense of belonging—to Nick's family, to Sunrise Island. And with it came a newfound autonomy, as if everything had finally fallen into place."I think I'm going to stay too," she replied, her voice steady, although they both knew it was no longer a question.

Nick smiled a slow, hopeful smile. He didn't press her for more or try to define what the future would hold. They would take it one day at a time, building something new out of the broken pieces.

As they stood side by side, Emily felt the weight of the past lift. There were still challenges ahead, still scars to heal, but for the first time in a long time, the future felt full of possibilities.

And that, she realized, was the true gift of Sunrise Island— a place where broken things could become whole again, where lost souls could find their way home.

* * *

Thank you for reading *Sunrise Island Christmas*. Stay tuned for the final book in the series, and remember to download *Cliff-house Footprints* so you know where it all began.

From beginning to end, the *Sunrise Island Series* invites readers into a world of friendship, love, and resilience centered around the island the Mitchell family calls home. Each carefully crafted story opens a window into the lives of women who face challenges, savour joys, and navigate moments both tender and tough.

I hope my books bring you laughter, inspiration, and perhaps a fresh perspective on the human experience. Thank you for joining me on this journey through Sunrise Island.

Bonus Recipe

CARROT PUDDING

1 1/4 cups grated raw carrot
1 1/2 cups grated apple, peeled
1 cup flour
2 tsp baking powder
1 tsp salt

½ tsp cloves
½ tsp nutmeg
½ tsp cinnamon
¼ cup butter
1 cup brown sugar
¾ cup seeded raisins
¼ cup grape juice
1 tsp baking soda

Grate carrots and apples separately and set aside. Reserve 1 tbs of flour to dust raisins.

Mix the remaining flour, baking powder, salt, cloves, nutmeg, and cinnamon.

Cream butter; gradually add brown sugar, beating well after each addition.

Add dry ingredients alternately with grape juice, blending well after each addition.

Add grated carrot, <u>half</u> of the grated apple, and all of the floured raisins.

Dissolve baking soda in remaining grated apple and add at once. Mix lightly.

Pour into greased 1 ½ quart mold. Cover tightly and steam
4½-5 hours.
Serve warm with hard sauce and lemon sauce. (Makes 6-8
servings)

HARD SAUCE

½ cup butter
¾ cup brown sugar
¾ cup icing sugar
1/3 cup whipping cream
1 tsp vanilla
2 tsp brandy (optional)

Cream butter, gradually add sugar; beat well
Slowly add whipping cream and vanilla, beating constantly
Pile into sauce dish
Make a well in centre. Add brandy and let sit until all
soaked up
Chill well before serving (Makes 1 ½ cups)

LEMON SAUCE

½ cup sugar
1 tbs cornstarch
Few grains of salt
½ tsp lemon rind
1 cup boiling water
2 tbs butter
1 ½ tbs lemon juice

Combine sugar, cornstarch, salt, and lemon rind in saucepan

Add boiling water gradually, stirring constantly

Cook and stir mixture over medium heat until clear and thickened—about 5 minutes

Remove from heat. Stir in butter and lemon juice. (Makes 1 cup)

MERRY
Christmas
AND HAPPY NEW YEAR

The Prequel

CLIFFHOUSE FOOTPRINTS
Book Description

Kathleen Mitchell longs to be a mother before her biological clock ticks out. After trying for two years, she and John consider adoption. She visualizes a newborn baby nestled in her arms, with skin as soft as the petals of a delicate flower. But when life takes an unexpected turn and Kathleen's eight-year-old nephew comes to live with them during his mother's battle with cancer, their plans are upended.

Amidst the emotional whirlwind of caregiving, Kathleen discovers profound truths about the essence of parental love—a love that transcends blood ties. From heartbreak to unexpected joys, their journey illuminates the transformative power of love and the resilience of the human spirit.

Cliffhouse Footprints, the Sunrise Island Series prequel, celebrates the undeniable force that drives parents to protect, nurture, and support their children through any circumstances.

Follow Kathleen in her transformative journey in this clean

women's fiction prequel, a celebration of those who care for children everywhere.

* * *

Scan the QR code to follow or see www.marenhill.com for details.

Be the first to know about new releases, cover reveals, discounts, giveaways, and outtakes from my life.

About the Author

Captivated by the intrigue of everyday life, Maren Hill writes heartfelt, emotional stories that celebrate women and the relationships that shape their lives.

Quirky, good-hearted characters you'd love to know, and stories laced with romance, humour, compassion, and inspiration are trademarks of Maren Hill's books.

<u>J.D. Monk</u>

Written by children's book author JD Monk, *Slimy Slick* appeals to both children and adults with fascinating facts about banana slugs.

If you enjoy my books, <u>please leave a review.</u> There's nothing more motivational than positive reviews. Thank you so much.

Also by Maren Hill

Cliffhouse Footprints

Cliffhouse by the Sea

Sunrise Island Sisters

Sunrise Island Christmas

Sunrise Island Celebrations

Nicole
The Troublemakers
Our Forever Place

Make a Spectacular Seashell Lamp
Sealed with a Kiss

What Readers Say

"Maren Hill's description of the island is so real that you can smell the salt air, feel the sand between your toes, the sun sparkling on the water, and hear the waves. Maren Hill weaves her stories extremely well."

"... she has a real knack for transporting the reader to the world of the story."

"The characters are great and the story is ... captivating."

"Awesome. Great setting, and relatable characters with solid backgrounds. Well written... character portrayal is solid with depth."

"... a suspenseful and mysterious story... will keep you on the edge of your seat."

"Excellent knack for transporting the reader into the world of the story... I can't wait for more. A true gem!"

"I thoroughly enjoyed ... Cliffhouse by the Sea... kept me wanting to know what would happen next."

"Maren Hill has done it again! Love this book. Would definitely read more by her."

"This story with Alexa and Kyla was riveting. I really enjoyed the dynamics of these two sisters. This is a great story."

"Beautifully done and exceptionally entertaining, heart-wrenching and delightful."

"Gorgeous writing! I love the author's rich descriptions of characters, scenes and situations - I felt like I was living it."

* * *

"JD Monk writes with a simplicity that pulls kids into the story immediately, but also with an underlying complexity and intelligence that allows the ideas in Slimy Slick to stay with them long after the tale ends. Well done!"

"This is a great story. Congratulations to the author for bringing awareness to these little creatures who are often misunderstood and undervalued. I love the education/entertainment combo. The illustrations are engaging and hilarious."

"Beautifully written and illustrated -- this is a wonderful bedtime story! Not only do we learn about the importance of banana slugs in our ecosystem in this story, but we're introduced to lovely language to increase the richness of our vocabulary. This is an awesome gift for children (and their parents) who are curious about their environment!"

"What a wonderful read! It was extremely informative about Banana Slugs; a very misunderstood creature. I learned a lot! The graphics are very well done! Definitely a must buy this Holiday Season for the little ones in the family!"

"Loved this book! Very well written, easy to understand and follow for children! Super informative as well, I had no idea slugs were this unique!"

"I have a whole new appreciation for slugs...The kids love it."

"... full of amazing facts about slugs... Completely recommend for curious kids who love nature."

"The fun facts were marvelous and very informative. 5 stars to the author. Highly recommend."

"Great book, full of lots of interesting slug facts. I recommend this for all young and young-at-heart bug lovers."

"Perfect for storytime and a wonderful way to explore nature!"

SLIMY SLICK—Not Just For Kids!

The Nighttime Adventures of a Banana Slug

This captivating picture book appeals to kids and adults through multiple reads and is jam-packed with suspense, slime, and fun facts.

Join Slimy Slick on his exciting nighttime adventure through the countryside as he glides toward the tasty treat of his dreams. He encounters an earthworm and a shrew, but the real danger lies ahead. Will Slick's journey come to an abrupt end at the hands of a well-meaning boy whose mission is to capture and eliminate? Does he not understand Slick's important role in the ecosystem?

Readers learn about the clever design of the banana slug and how Slick uses his natural gifts to protect himself and navigate life in the wild.

Discover the world of Slimy Slick through a rainforest adventure that educates and entertains, emphasizing the importance of these fascinating creatures to our planet.

Perfect for:

• Parents and grandparents, science teachers, librarians, educators

• Gifts for kids who love nature, rainforest animals, and learning more about the natural world and zoology

• Read-aloud family sharing

• Gaining environmental wisdom

• Understanding empathy and collaboration

Acknowledgments

I extend my heartfelt thanks to **Jane Litherland** and **Terri Morgans** for their exceptional editing services and to **Beverley Sparks** and **Stephanie Ferguson** for their steadfast support and encouragement. I am deeply grateful for my family, whose love has been the anchor that kept me grounded through every creative storm.

www.ingramcontent.com/pod-product-compliance
Lightning Source LLC
Chambersburg PA
CBHW051232210726
48290CB00003B/919